Napata Rising
A Novella

Marcella Denise Spencer

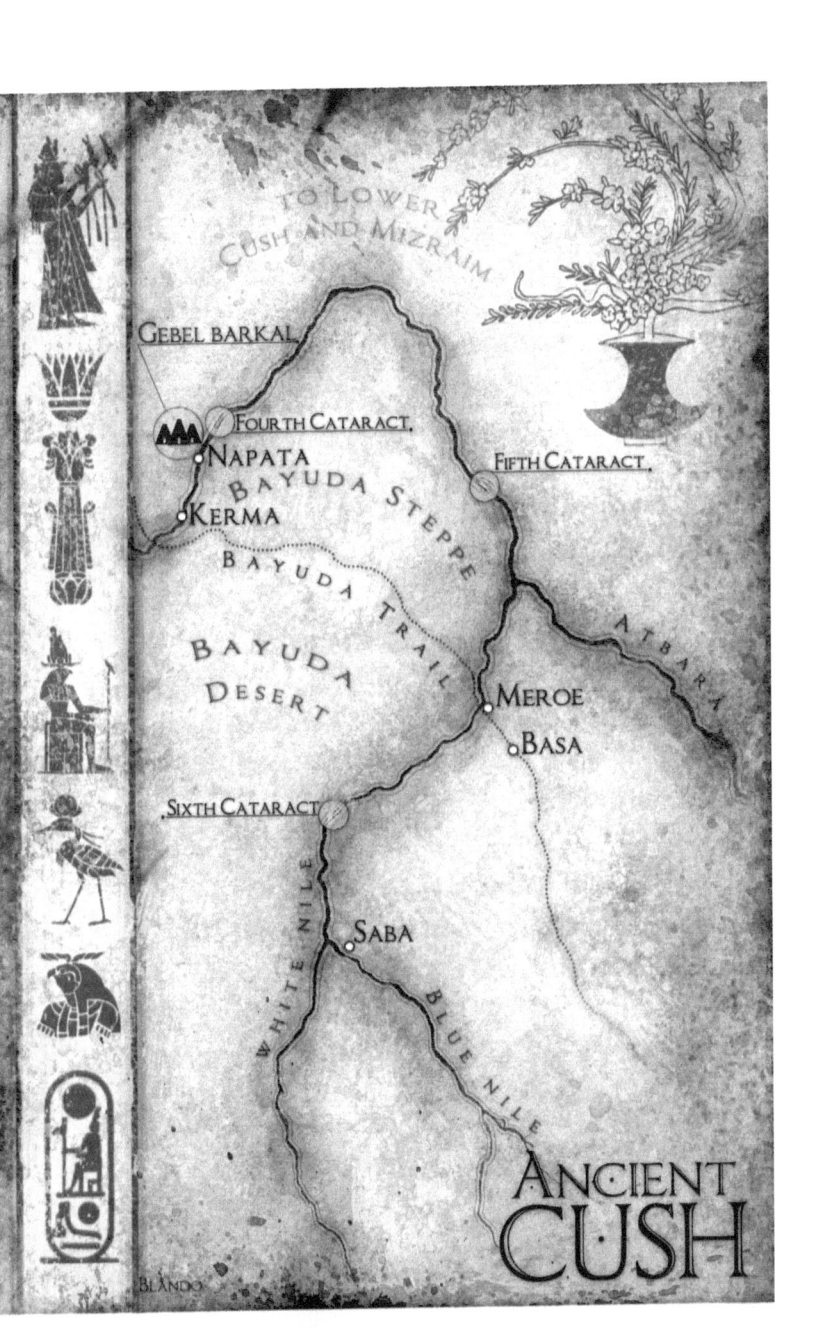

TO LOWER
CUSH AND MIZRAIM

GEBEL BARKAL

FOURTH CATARACT

NAPATA

FIFTH CATARACT

KERMA

BAYUDA STEPPE

BAYUDA TRAIL

ATBARA

BAYUDA
DESERT

MEROE

BASA

SIXTH CATARACT

WHITE NILE

SABA

BLUE NILE

ANCIENT
CUSH

BLANDO

One

The summons came after the midday ritual. He had been expecting it. He knew that he could not continue to function in this manner before someone noticed. What he did not expect was his composure.

When the courier handed him the letter, in front his colleagues, Ay, the Second Prophet of Amon, smoothed imaginary wrinkles from his white linen kilt, handed his papyrus roll on which sloppy but accurate offerings to the god were noted, and left. His demeanor suggested that being ordered to stand before the High Priest in Meroe was a daily occurrence.

The Second Prophet was deputy to the High Priest, responsible for the offerings made to the temple from royal estates, overseeing the temple administrators, and taking care of the temple's economy. His revenue came from the temple's prosperity, its daily offerings and the success of its crops. After the god, Amon-Ra, consumed the offerings of food, beer and wine the remaining bounty could be passed to the priests.

Ay would take home no trussed ducks, beef, bread, fish, nor any fruits and vegetables this day.

Ay relieved his full bladder before walking down the temple's quay to a boat. He traveled in silence, making no conversation with the temple worker who sailed the vessel. On his arrival, he sat on a stone bench outside the High Priest's office; its hard coldness seeped through his white linen kilt. His palms rested on his knees. While a harpist played music to the god, Ay wondered about his punishment. A *sem*-priest, cloaked in a leopard skin cape came forward and gestured for Ay to follow. The Second Prophet rose on thick, steady legs. He felt calm. He needed a drink, but he felt calm.

After the meeting, the High Priest escorted Ay past the rectangular Sacred Lake. Long shadows covered the temple's stone floors as golden sunlight streamed through the lotus- decorated columns. Ay wondered at his superior's thoughtfulness. *Does he extend this honor to every priest he demotes? And where are we going? The quay is in the opposite direction.*

They strolled down the temple's processional way, passing two bare-chested priests, also dressed in white kilts, who spoke to each other in angry, hushed tones. They separated at the passing of two high-ranking priests, evident by the tattoos on their right arms, and lowered their heads in submission.

The High Priest laid a hand on Ay's bare shoulder. "Ay, you have been in the priesthood for many summers. You have made friends and formed connections. Therefore, do not fret. You may restore your loss of income in other ways."

Ay turned watery eyes to him. "Indeed?" The priest smiled, nodding yes.

***

Kerit-Amon leveled narrowed eyes at her husband. "You drunken fool! We are the talk of Meroe, the disgrace of Cush."

Ay stretched his hands toward her. "My dear, you exaggerate. The demotion is temporary, I shall return to my position as Second Prophet by the next inundation."

"How? You are disfavored, Ay, by your superiors..." she picked up a carved ebony figurine and aimed it at him. Ay leaped out of the way. "And by me." The figurine hit the wall and fell to the floor in pieces.

Nekhti, their oldest daughter stood trapped between the front room, where her parents fought, and her room. She tiptoed across the floor and up the staircase.

"What manner are we to live in now, Ay? What does a Fourth Prophet bring home from temple? A loaf of stale bread? Surely, no wineskins."

"No, dear, no more wineskins. Temporarily."

She snorted. "Temporarily. You are a failure. This family will never gain any prominence with you as the head."

"Kerit-Amon, it is you who drives me to drink. You and your ambitions..."

She interrupted him. "Me? The only thing that I try to drive you to do is to succeed at something. Now you are a failure. What shall we do now, Ay?"

"I shall continue farming, I did well before I – before *you* decided that I should devote time to the priesthood." He smiled weakly. "Farming is all I ever wanted to do."

Kerit-Amon let out a long, exasperated wail.

Nekhti heard her father mount the stairs. He would sleep on the roof tonight, she knew.

***

The following afternoon Nekhti sat a basket filled with warm honey cakes into the back of the family's mule cart, climbed aboard and drove to the home of her best friend Sissi. Both girls were the oldest daughters of priests, Sissi's father serving as the High Priest in the Meroe's main temple. The mule plodded down a gravel road along the Nile River lined with acacia trees.

A woman with her hair plaited in multiple tiny braids sat outside her home picking early cucumbers. Nekhti turned right down a street lined with mud-brick homes. Cows grazed behind gated fields, goats bleated from enclosed pens in the rear of homes, and dogs ran, barking among children at play.

To her left, she could see a goose and her goslings waddling down the Nile's bank. A man swore loudly as he tried to coax his ox from its pen out to the fields. Nekhti chuckled, surprised by her lightness of spirit despite her family's problem. Her father's demotion would affect their livelihood and the marriage prospects of her and her younger sister, Neferua.

She would not dwell on such dour thoughts this day. She was going to visit her friend Sissi, and enjoy the afternoon, hopeful that everything would turn out well. It had too, for she had decided long ago to marry well.

And nothing, not even father's misfortune would turn her away from such a goal.

She arrived at a two-story home bordered by incense trees and disembarked.

Nekhti sighed as she brushed the breadcrumbs off her frock. "I thought I would be a wife by the time your baby arrived." She said scooting back against a palm's trunk.

Sissi rubbed her extended belly and sighed with contentment. She smiled at her best friend, whose dreamy brown eyes were now filled with anxiety. "Your prince has not yet arrived. He was supposed to appear dressed in gold, yes?" They sat outside Sissi's home, finishing the midday meal.

"Aye, and he is to speed into the village in a golden chariot."

"Do not forget his team of groomed white stallions, trained and bred on the Dongola."

"Oh, yes." The girls snickered. "And, he will take me away from here."

"To Napata…" Sissi finished.

"Yes, to Napata, where I will live in a house as big as any of Meroe's nobles."

Sissi hoisted herself off the ground and walked about. "Must he be a prince?"

Nekhti stood, flung her cloak around her shoulders, and started prancing. "Only a prince would do for My Majesty."

Sissi laughed. "My Nekhti. When you marry your prince and move to Napata, who will keep me in good humor?"

Nekhti dropped to her knees. "Your baby. You will visit me in Napata, will you not?"

"Indeed, I must see that your prince is treating you well."

Nekhti looked away; she rubbed the hardened skin on her hand. "How do you expect my mother to react if I marry well?"

"You mean *when*, do you not?"

"Yes, *when* I marry well."

"I doubt whether she would treat you any differently. She will probably be jealous that you married above her."

"Jealousy. I had never considered that. You do not think that she will be happy for me?"

Sissi shook her head slowly. "No. But I will be happy for you."

"I know you will, my friend."

They were quiet for a moment. "How is your mother?"

"The same. Furious that she is now the wife of a lowly priest. She cannot decide whether to move out of the village or stay."

"Why would she consider moving? Is that not extreme?"

Nekhti nodded yes, now conscious how deep the family pride was. "She is embarrassed. As am I. I wish my prince would make haste; it is my desire to leave as soon as possible."

***

Temple Karnak
Waset, Kham

Katep slammed the reed pen on the ink palette and leaned his back against the stone wall. Turning his head, he looked out at the Nile River; high during this the second month of summer. A beautiful evening had arrived in Waset. The sun had crept behind the sandstone-colored mountains, leaving streaks of lavender and pink in the sky.

Palm trees along the riverbank waved gently. The breeze carried evening meal preparations up to Katep's open balcony. Roasting fowl, leeks, and garlic aromas made his stomach growl.

Torches were lighting across the city. Boats, skiffs and papyrus canoes dodged one another for space in the harbor.

Katep heard a soft rustling noise outside his curtained doorway; he turned to see a female figure passed with a stack of papyrus scrolls under her arm. Khensa. What an appetite she had for the written word, more so than any female he'd heard of before.

With a sigh, he picked up the pen again and resumed writing in hieratic.

Kings promoted sons who became High Priests. Violence broke out. Brother fought against brother, all vying for the double crown. At last High Priest, Osorkon, and his brother crushed the rebellious members in their dynasty.

"Enemies were suppressed who were within this land, which had sunk into confusion at this time."

When Katep finished, he threw the pen across the limestone floor. The Chronicles of Prince Osorkon were now complete. Kham had survived this uncivilized ascension of the present king, now known as Osorkon III. *But...*Katep closed his eyes.

The Libyans had to go. Like the kings of old who removed the enemy from the Two Lands, a leader had to do the same now so that the priesthood could again become influential. There is one problem: Takeloth, High Priest of Amon. Libyan, son of king Osorkon. The position should be mine. But how? Who could help remove them from power? There is no Ahmose I, whose golden battle-axe drove the Hyksos from Kham. No Thutmosis III or Ramesses the Great.

Katep stroked his chin, recalling the lavish celebrations in Cush that marked the new monarch's coronation. Could he convince King Kashta to align with him in his efforts to secure the position of High Priest?

Katep pushed the chronicles aside, reached for the papyrus roll and tore off a fresh piece, then fished around in his leather sack for another pen. He dipped the pen in the ink. *Careful. A veiled query, it should give no hint at treason.*

A tap-tap sounded on the doorframe. Katep looked up to see a familiar face peek around the curtain. He blew the sheet before turning it over. "Come in."

"I see that you are still hard at work," Sen-nefer said, entering.

"Indeed. I have finished the Chronicles of Prince Osorkon," Katep sneered, unable to hide his displeasure.

Sen-nefer raised his kilt and sat on the low cedar table. "A sordid tale. The Two Lands have had better reigns." He leaned in and plucked a purple grape from a cluster in an alabaster bowl.

"Only moments ago I was thinking the same. Ahmose I, Thutmosis III, Ramesses the Great."

"They were royal brethren, true sons of Amon." Sen-nefer lowered his voice, "Not impostors."

"How often, in the last few summers, have we had this conversation?"

Katep watched Sen-nefer closely, wondering whether he could trust the Third Prophet. "I have an idea."

Sen-nefer's black eyes danced.

***

Twenty-one sunrises later, two priests walked in solemn companionship through the marketplace. The morning brightness had faded; the market brimmed with bare-footed women in long, white frocks. Many carried a baby on their backs; others had their hands occupied with produce-filled baskets. The screams of upset children, and the vendors crying out their wares, allowed the priests to speak in private.

"How do we fare?" Sen-nefer asked.

"Our query to Cush has suffered a setback," Katep said.

Sen-nefer turned to his superior with concerned eyes. "Sir?"

Katep raised a sandaled foot, missing the fast approach of a wooden ball. A child ran forward, ducking between Katep's legs, in pursuit of his toy. The priest gripped Sen-nefer's shoulder to steady himself. "A colleague has sent word that correspondence addressed to Cush has been discussed."

"Discussed? By the Vizier's agents?" Sen-nefer said in a fierce whisper.

"Indeed," Katep said. "Our status is precarious at present. Finding that letter is a priority."

***

Grand Vizier Pamiu *knew* that something was amiss. At daybreak, he stood at the river's edge, listening to the Nile, eyes closed. The king's servant was dressed in a short, white kilt and wore a solid gold collar around his neck. When he opened his eyes, he marveled anew at the perfection before him, how the Nile's shimmery blue blended effortlessly with the pale sandy banks and the emerald palm leaves.

Pamiu was not fooled, though. Ma'at, the harmony which governed Kham, was disturbed again. He intended to discover not only why...but by whom.

It was Pamiu's job to know all that is and is not in Kham. Pamiu was the eyes of the Great House, Grand Vizier for the present king, Osorkon III, and his father Takeloth II. When he returned to his villa, his aide handed him several papyrus sheets, messages from his Wasetian agents. They reported nothing unusual, but the delta agents would be reporting in soon

He climbed the stairs to the roof and stared out at the city. The sun shone bright as midday approached. In the distance, he could see the high walls of Karnak, where the High Priest Takeloth III would soon be washing in the Sacred Lake. Once clean, he would enter the inner sanctuary and tend the god with prayers and food sacrifices.

Pamiu smelled the roasted duck being prepared by his cook in the open kitchen below. He hoped Cook remembered to use the parsley and thyme sparingly; too much gave him a rather uncomfortable reaction.

The Vizier watched the river as several barges floated up the Nile, returning to Karnak. Bare-chested scribes sat inside each barge, with detailed notes of the amount of grain to be collected from the farmers for taxes. The grain would be stored in the temple granaries for the god Amon, or if a shortage occurred in the land.

"Grand Vizier." Pamiu turned to see a delta based courier standing in the doorway, holding a papyrus sheet. "Your immediate attention is required."

Two

Osorkon III, king of Kham, stood in front of the Bubasite gate at Karnak and ran his hand across the wall's decoration. The city, Bubastis, in the eastern delta, was where Osorkon's people had settled during the reign of Ramesses II. Osorkon let his finger trace the image of his ancestor, Sheshonq I, being nursed by the goddess Hathor. This predecessor, had defied the odds in his climb to power, and brought the Libyan people to prominence in a land they had entered as slaves.

Osorkon understood that animosity remained between Khamites and Libyans, two peoples who had long been enemies.

The king would admit that his dynasty did not do much to improve their favor. Some forty summers after Sheshonq I took the throne, his descendants continuously fought one another for power, bringing bloodshed and instability to the Two Lands.

Pictured on the wall, standing next to Sheshonq I was his son, the High Priest Iuwelot. Osorkon did not trace Iuwelot's image. Instead, he turned to the Grand Vizier and thanked him for the information. The letter retrieved by his delta agents was proof enough to Osorkon that Kham still did not care for Libyans'; especially one who sat on the throne.

***

Takeloth II, High Priest of Amon at Karnak, hurried away from his walled estate. *What could be amiss? It cannot be good news that brings Father to the south now.* He leaped into the waiting chariot and headed for the royal palace. He saw few people along this route, his mansion being in a secluded section of Waset. Takeloth spotted the occasional gardener or estate caretaker as his chariot sped by.

As the driver arrived in town, the traffic became more congested, and most people congregated in shady areas. A boy herded cattle through the streets. The chariot's progress slowed as it drew closer to the palace. People heading to and from market crossed in the vehicle's path, forcing the driver to completely stop at times.

King Osorkon rarely visited his home in the south. The king and his court preferred the delta area in Lower Kham, specifically Tanis. The king came to the Southland for important religious festivals. When Takeloth learned of his father's arrival, he could not finish his morning meal. For a moment, he considered delaying his departure to the palace, but the royal courier's eyes brooked no debate. *Something was wrong*.

When he arrived at the palace, Takeloth went straight to his father's office. Armed guards stood on both sides of the door. Takeloth rapped twice on the door frame. The herald appeared, turned toward the king, and announced Takeloth's arrival.

"Come in, Takeloth," said the king.

"Father, you wanted to see me?"

"Yes." Osorkon sat in an open space between two columns, oblivious to the blanket of heat. He went to his desk and picked up a papyrus sheet, then handed it to Takeloth. "Read this correspondence. Tell me what you make of it."

Takeloth took his time reading the letter. Finally, he said, "It is delightfully cryptic. A message to someone in Cush."

"Yes."

"Truly?" He head shot up. "Where did you get it?"
Takeloth reread the letter. "It is not especially addressed to
the Great House. However, the salutation is for a nobleman."

"The salutation is for a king." Osorkon came from
around his desk to look at the letter again. He pointed to a
Sparrow Hawk, the royal insignia of Cush.

"I suppose it could be a conspiracy. There are still
murmurs about the Libyan element in the Great House.
How we have brought shame to the Black Land. What are
your suspicions, Father?"

"That someone in the priesthood wants me removed
from power. Why else summon Cush?"

"As if they had no turmoil or civil unrest before we arrived. Kham for Khamites, yes I have heard this before.
This is the first time, though, that I have seen direct action
taken on the matter. I shall be on alert."

"Please do."

"May I borrow the letter, Sir? I would like to compare
the writing with my priests and scribes."

Osorkon nodded. "Excellent idea. Prepare to depart to
Tanis, I have scheduled a meeting."

Takeloth bowed and backed out of the room.

***

In the delta city of Tanis, a meeting convened in the
king's audience room. The eight men sitting in front of
King Osorkon sipped beer from drinking bowls. Osorkon,
recently returned from Kham, stood before them holding a
goblet of date-palm wine. He cleared his throat and spoke.

"From the Bedouin chieftain to the king occupying the
hallowed palace halls in Asshur, every leader has a fear.
And that fear is of an uprising. The loss of power, the end

to his dynasty and everything he has built. Our deeds are erased from memory; our names are never mentioned in the afterlife.

The biggest threats to a peaceful Kham are more uprising from the malcontents in my dynasty, whom I will monitor, and a unified Kham and Cush. Both lands under one crown would undermine the progress the Libyan people have made since we arrived here as slaves. This must not occur. I permit Grand Vizier Pamiu," the king nodded to the narrow-faced Egyptian to his left, "to employ a heavy hand against all suspects forming a conspiracy along these concerns.

More specifically, Grand Vizier, I need you and your agents to monitor Cushite activity in Kham."

***

Today was an unholy day, the fourteenth of Tybi, when Isis and Nephthys mourned for Osiris. Inside the Drunken Goose Tavern, Sebni, its owner, kept his eye on the smooth-faced stranger sitting alone in the corner. He wanted no foolishness in his establishment this day. Sebni reclined on a three-legged stool, with his thick legs spread apart. There were six men in the tavern, bare-chested and wearing white kilts, except for the stranger.

His undershirt had an embroidered collar, a sure sign to Sebni that this man with the long legs was neither artisan, metal worker, nor a laborer in the quarry, but from the noble classes. What was he doing in this part of Mennefer? The dark brown-skinned stranger sat on one of the many papyrus-woven mats strewn across the dirt floor, drinking beer and eating salted watermelon seeds.

The stranger's attention was fixed on the game of draughts. The players were two of Sebni's best customers,

Uni, the chief workman at the limestone quarry in Terofu, against Khonsumose, an artisan. Both men played in silence, their brows knitted in concentration. Because no merriment was allowed on this unluckiest of days, Sebni appreciated his patrons' soberness; it allowed him to feel less guilty about opening for business today.

Sebni brought the stool down with a thud, then stood and plodded around the room. "Nebnofr, my friend, are you in needof a refill?" He patted the patron's bare shoulder, peering into his cup.

"So I can stagger home? No, thanks, Sebni, you know how the wife feels about that."

Sebni chuckled. He came near the stranger, and for a moment pretended to be engrossed in the game. Then he said, "Are you new to Men-nefer?"

The stranger looked up at the man's fleshly, dark bronze face. The black kohl on the owner's eyelids had smeared from perspiration. "No, Sir, though it is my first time in your fine establishment. The name is Khaliut."

Sebni, rarely spoken to in such polite terms, took an instant liking to the man. "Khaliut, is it? My name is Sebni, and as you have guessed, I am the owner of this place."

Khaliut nodded his head, agreeing.

"You are from Men-nefer?"

"No. Waset."

Sebni snorted. "Not many people are natives in this country nowadays. At least not here in the lower parts."

"True," Khaliut said, he took a sip of his beer, keeping his eye on the chunky tavern owner.

"Foreigners, everywhere you turn. Kham for Khamites that is the way it should be. Has not been that way for a long time. Not that I have anything against foreigners…"

"It is all the fault of the Ramessides, you know," Khonsumose piped in.

"Of course it is," Sebni said. "Ramesses the Second started it by bringing those *tchenu* slaves from Libya and elsewhere. And where do they drop all those foreigners?" He eyed each of his patrons, to see whether any knew the answer. He turned to Khaliut and pointed downward with his finger. "Here. In the Delta. Always in the Delta. You never see any foreigners brought to Waset, do you?"

Uni, Khonsumose and two other men shook their heads no. Khonsumose waited until Uni made his move on the board before adding, "And those Libyans, since they have been free, do nothing but grope for power."

"Parasites!" Sebni said.

Khaliut took his time, looking into each man's eyes. How passionate were these men? What do they think about the fate of their country, the land of Ham built and maintained by their ancestors. And how far would any of them go to restore it?

"You heard about what happened to Mekhuw?" Uni said. The men shook their heads shamefully, sorry about what had happened to Mekhuw.

"What has happened to your friend, Mekhuw?" Khaliut asked Sebni.

A muscle in the tavern owner's jaw twitched. Moments passed before he spoke. "They nearly beat him to death."

"They?"

"Agents working for Pamiu," someone added.

Sebni cast a suspicious eye at Khaliut. "Where are you from exactly? Have you any idea the condition this country is in?"

"I do, Sir. What was Mekhuw's occupation? Was there any reason for the attack?"

"What does his occupation have to do with anything? The Libyans, now running this country do not care for any man's position." Sebni shrugged. "Do not misunderstand me, I have nothing against foreigners, but they do not know how to run Kham. They are making a mockery out of us. But to answer your question, he was a letter carrier. And they beat him soundly, and went off with the correspondence he was supposed to deliver." Sebni turned to Uni. "How does his family fare?"

"Rumor has it that they are moving to Waset, after Mekhuw's recovery," said Uni.

"I suppose that is best. They probably will fare better to live in a district, mostly Khamitic. Do not misunderstand me, now, I have nothing against foreigners, but the clergy know how to run Waset better than anyone."

"And why should they not?" said Khonsumose. "They have been doing it for centuries." The men laughed. Sebni turned to Khaliut to see whether he understood the jest. The stranger had gone.

***

A few days later, shortly after dawn, someone banged on the servants' door at the royal palace in Tanis. Bint-Anath, called Binty by her friends, held a basket of pomegranates. She threw a hateful glance at the door. *What goose is calling now?* The banging resumed. Binty slammed the basket down on a table. "By the head of Horus!" She unlatched the fence with force.

"Good morning, fair lady."

Binty deflated. "What are you selling at this ungodly hour?"

"I have some freshly picked barley for the palace. I know how the king loves his porridge, so I thought that it might please him on this day."

"Truly." Binty squinted her eyes at him. "I have not seen you around here before."

"No, my lady. I am Anen. I usually do business in other districts, the competition being so fierce here in Tanis."

"Yes, yes. Come in and show me what you have." She stepped back to let him in. The merchant heaved two baskets on the table, one filled with barley and the other with onions. Binty grabbed each onion by its stalk, and eyed it for bruising, then squeezed the bulb for firmness.

"What is on the mind of our king these days?" the merchant asked.

"I am the cook, Sir, not the Vizier."

He barked a laugh. "Yes, of course. Our peers do talk, yes? I believe that it is as important for us among the peasant classes to remain informed."

Binty looked up at the lanky stranger, then nodded in assent. "Truly, I will know shortly when the king's steward comes down to order his majesty's meal." With all the onions laid out and inspected, Binty went through the barley with the same care. Finally, she said, "I will give you a jug of freshly brewed beer and some loaves of bread."

"Thank you, fair lady."

Bint-Anath blushed. "You can call me Binty. Wait right here."

Binty returned a few moments later, relieved to find the merchant in the same spot as she had left him. She did not care for strangers in her kitchen. Usually, she was not so inconvenienced, because the palace gardens produced adequate foodstuffs. Why today? Well, he was a charming

lad, was he not? Should the king want his favorite porridge, there was no time to lay it before him this fresh.

"Here you are, Sir." Binty said, placing a jug of beer
into one of the merchant's baskets and stuffing the other
basket with bread loaves.

"I thank you for your hospitality, Binty. I am forced
to do business discreetly, for I have heard that the Libyans
have resorted to force against Cushites in Kham, such das-
tardly behavior. Rumor has it that a mail carrier was as-
saulted under this new policy."

Binty's eyes grew stormy. "Tis my son they harmed."

Khaliut widened his eyes in shock. "My dear lady,
how full of care you must have been. Tell me about it."

***

The moment Khaliut arrived in Waset, he stopped in at
an apartment in Karnak temple to bathe and shave. This
apartment, thought to be a mere storeroom, was kept for his
use. Wearing a fresh kilt and reed sandals, Khaliut headed
for a small village on the Nile's eastern bank, right outside
the temple.

Khaliut circled the village on a donkey. On his second
trip around, a woman came out of the last hut on the row,
dragging a mortar and pestle behind her. Placing the mortar firmly between her feet, she began to grind. Khaliut
halted the donkey nearby, and slid off the animal's back.
Leaning close to its ear, Khaliut spoke to it as he watched
the woman's awkward pounding.

She wore a dress that would burst if she bent too
suddenly, and a shoulder-length wig. Her feet were excep-
tionally long and slender, with no adornments on either an-
kle. She did wear bronze bangles, which jangled with each
stab. Her kohl-lined eyelids were smattered with gold dust.

"Has the letter been retrieved?" She said without looking up.

"No. Your informant proved correct. The letter was taken from a carrier in Men-nefer. The poor lad had been beaten."

The woman stopped and leaned on the pestle. "By Mut, how did it end up in Men-nefer? Says much about our mail system, does it not? " She pounded with such force, Khaliut thought the mortar would split.

Khaliut told her what he learned in Men-nefer and Ta-nis. "Why beat the lad?"

The woman seemed thoughtful. "Yes, why indeed? Something else is going on."

Khaliut removed a bowl from the bridle sack and walked toward the well. When he returned he asked. "What are my orders?"

"You are to go to Cush."

Khaliut lowered the bowl and let the donkey drink. "What is at stake?"

"The end of Kham, as we know it and as our fathers did." The woman grunted. "Do you think it coincidence that Kham is weak, yet Ta-Seti is strong? It is an act of the gods."

"A strong Cush?" Khaliut kept his expression blank. "We have never been good to our southern brethren. Is there anyone in the south who would sympathize?"

"That is what you will learn. A dynasty has arisen, a family of warriors. Not an uncommon event in Cush, but a useful one for Kham now."

Khaliut picked up the empty bowl and put it back in the sack. The woman stopped pounding and used her fo-rearm to wipe the perspiration from her brow. She let out a few expletives. "This is harsh work. I shall be more tolerant of the bread maker."

Khaliut lowered his head, hiding a smile.

"Your orders, more especially, are to make yourself a *home* in Cush, Napata to be precise." The woman stole a sideward glance at Khaliut. She had stressed the word home, but he did not seem to hear.

"Whom am I to observe?"

"The nobility. King Kashta. Go to festive gatherings..." Khaliut grimaced. "Whisper in the ears of highborn women, military officers, priests... and see whom we can count on for support."

Khaliut mounted his donkey. "And our contact there?"

"She will contact you."

Khaliut raised his brows. "She?"

The woman tossed her braids. "What? Do you have something against women?"

"No, of course not."

"Good. Life, health, and prosperity to you," said the woman.

"And the same to you."

The "woman," Katep, Second Prophet of Amon, threw the pestle on the ground and went inside to get out of that frock.

Three

Khaliut eyed the greenish-brown back of the crocodile, with its head resting on the river's bank and its tail in the water. He regarded the animal with the same curiosity he had toward this first trip to Cush. *I know nothing about this land. Only that it is in my blood. Will I feel different after entering Cush? Will anybody know of me? Shall I finally meet the father I have never known?*

He had boarded *The Tame Bull* at Wawat in northern Cush. The foremost gold producing region in the Nile Valley, Wawat's natural resources had funded wars, expeditions, and the building of palaces for the kings of Kham. Khamite occupation of Wawat during the Middle Kingdom, and again in the New Kingdom, had caused dissension with their neighbor and brethren, Cush.

The wooden boat passed acacia forests, gold mines, and dark-skinned natives, clad in loincloths, tending cattle. Khaliut's eyes widened at the sight of Cush's largest temple, Abu Simbel. Carved out of solid sandstone, four huge images of Ramesses II flanked the temple's entrance.

The Nile began an "S" bend at the third cataract, leading into Upper Cush toward Napata. A wind gust lifted Khaliut's white head-cloth. He felt an anxious surge and gripped the ship's railing. For a moment, he stood facing the limestone cliffs. Then he returned to his seat, unable to admit defeat but still not ready to see Cush.

***

A small stone temple sat on the outskirts of Meroe. At midday, five weeks after his departure, Khaliut stood opposite the temple waiting for his contact. Dressed in a short linen skirt and sandals, he leaned against a brick building, drinking water from a used wineskin. He wore a short-plaited wig. A cloak covered him from head to foot, shielding his facial features.

Palms heavy with fruit grew on both sides of the colonnaded temple. A monkey sat on a tree limb, watching the human beings. Bald priests entered the temple. Women walked past with children in tow. A mule cart with a broken wheel rumbled down the dirt road.

A woman with a shawl covering her face drew near him. She held a papyrus slip in her hand. She looked up at the building and down at her slip. "You are the Khamite?"

"Indeed." Khaliut straightened. "What word do you have for me?"

"You speak well. Are you a nobleman?"

"Nay, my lady. I am a royal courier."

She slipped the papyrus into her shawl. "Relaying messages is a full-time occupation. How do you find time to gather intelligence?"

Khaliut stared straight ahead. "One always finds time for things that matter. And you?" He looked into her half-veiled eyes, then at her frock.

Her eyes grew stormy at his scrutiny. "My family is related to the Great House."

Khaliut raised a brow. "Truly? How so?"

She lifted her chin. "My father is a cousin of the late king Alara."

"How keen. What do you know?"

"Osorkon has a new policy against Cushites in Kham. He fears something."

What? What does Osorkon fear? And how did she come about this information? Khaliut waited for a response; she gave nothing but a sly smile. He bowed deep. "Good day to you." He walked away.

The woman frowned at his back. *How dare he look at me as if I were a peasant. I am the second daughter of a high-ranking priest. I was, but now, yes, now I am the daughter of a farmer.* She stamped her foot. *I do not intend to remain so. This intelligence business serves one purpose, to get me close to a royal brother, for nothing less than a noble marriage.* She turned and headed toward the temple to collect her wage.

Khaliut waited until she entered the temple, then followed. He watched as she spoke to a portly priest with watery eyes, and saw her lips mouth a fraternal greeting. Then she approached a man whose attire and makeup seemed elaborate, even for a Cushite. He wore gold bands on his upper arms, gold bangles around his wrist, long turquoise earrings hanging from his ears, and heavy kohl lining his eyelids.

Khaliut had seen men in Kham wear braided female wigs, but this man's plaits had multicolored beads. And he was fair-skinned.

Khaliut waited behind a column during the god's afternoon ministrations. He smelled the heady incense from where he stood.

Moments passed, and priests filed out of the temple. When a bald man of medium built came stumbling out, Khaliut came from behind the column, taking the stairs down two at a time. "Friend," he said to the man stagger-

ing before him. "May I help you home?" Khaliut placed
his hand on the man's elbow.

"Why, thank you, Sir, but I know this route like the lines
on the palm of my own hand. No need to bother."

Khaliut turned his head away, briefly, for fresh air. The
priest's kilt sat askew; the right side had slipped down his
waist. "No bother, sir. Are you not the Fourth Prophet?"

"Yes, sir. I was the Second Prophet. Would have been
high priest had my fortune not changed."

"That must have been a great loss for your family."

"Indeed, sir. The wife promises never to forgive me,
and when that woman determines to do…" The priest
shook his head. "Are you a priest, sir? From Napata, I
suspect."

"No, Prophet, though I am familiar with the priesthood.
You have children, yes?"

"Indeed I do, sir. I have two daughters, one of my heart
and body. The other, well, I have known her all my life,
yet she is but a stranger. Her mother's child," he said nodding his head. His eyes brightened. "Ah, but my Nekhti.
She is my real daughter." He looked around then lowered
his voice. "I think her younger sister is someone else's.
Have we met before?"

"No, Prophet. I have that kind of face."

"Here I am," the Prophet pointed to a village, a cluster
of two-storied homes. "Listen, come in and have a meal
with us."

"Thank you, Prophet."

The priest wagged an awkward finger in Khaliut's face.
"You are somebody." His hand dropped to his side. "Me?
I am nobody now, something that my wife will never let me
forget."

"Not true, sir. Your family is kin to nobility, is it not?"

"No. Nobody." They walked in silence for a moment, then the Prophet began to cry.

Khaliut glanced about, anxiously. "Prophet, what ails you?"

The prophet looked up at Khaliut with red-rimmed eyes; then pointed to a house. "I am home."

***

Nekhti set the bucket on the sandy bank. She massaged the rough skin on her right hand and stared across the water. Two skiffs floated past, bobbing side by side down the Nile. A bigger vessel, owned by richer people, sailed toward Napata.

Nekhti followed the ship with her eyes until it became too small to see. *Fifteen summers old and I have never been to Napata.* She let out a heavy sigh, and looked down at her empty bucket.

I am now a farmer's daughter. I suppose it would be worse if I had been born a farmer's daughter. She chuckled. *Actually, I was. Father never wanted to join the priesthood. But I am no longer the daughter of the Second Prophet.*

Nekhti looked around to see whether anybody was about, then began walking on the tips of her toes. *But, oh to be royal, that has always been my dream. One day a royal official will come and invite father, mother, sister and me to the palace.*

"Did you not know, Nekhti," father would say, *"that we are royal relations. Did you not know that I joined the priesthood to prepare for the throne?"* Nekhti did a final twirl and curtsied. She straightened, grabbed the bucket, dipped it into the river and headed home.

Her village lay on the outskirts of Meroe, an ancient town in southern Cush. According to legend, the first inhabitants of Waset in Kham migrated there from Meroe. The prosperous district was home to priests and military families who all occupied two-story homes. Nekhti could see the roofs of red-brick, and tall colonnaded buildings in Meroe from her rooftop.

She often imagined herself living elsewhere. When her family went to town, Nekhti paid close attention to the caravans that traveled along the Atbara River. *Where were they going?* She would wonder aloud, much to the annoyance of her sister. *Who would wear the gold, carnelian, and panther skins that the caravans brought?*

To the east were the tombs of Cush's kings; at least five dynasties rested there. Meroe also boasted of grand estates occupied by palace officials and high-ranking military officers.

"Nekhti," her mother said on her return, "what took you so long? You were not required to make the water, just to gather some from the river."

Nekhti raised her eyes to meet her mother's scowl. "Sorry, Mother."

"We have a guest. Go and wash the sand from your feet." Nekhti rushed off to do as told. Once clean, she entered the courtyard kitchen. Her mother removed the roasted goose from the spit. Nekhti went to get the big reed platter for the meat. Her younger sister, Neferua, was in the eating area, placing fresh dates on the table.

"I did some farming myself before the position in the priesthood became vacant," Nekhti's father was saying. "My father was a priest, and my grandfather a high priest. Grandfather was once summoned by our late king Alara, himself."

"Is that so?" Khaliut said. "To be schooled in two professions, sir, you are fortunate." Nekhti caught some drippings from the goose into a small bowl. She paused when she heard the guest's voice. She had never heard such cultured speech before.

"I love farming," Khaliut said. "I hope to learn from your expertise."

"Nekhti, quit your daydreaming," said her mother. "Take the drippings and the bread to the table."

Nekhti ran a hand over her short-cropped hair. She knew once she saw this guest of her father, she would know whether he was high born. She could always spot nobility.

"Here she is," her father said. "Sir, may I present to you my oldest child, Nekhti."

Nekhti set the bowl and breadbasket on the table. She straightened and curtsied, certain there must be a misunderstanding. The lanky, handsome stranger with his erect posture could not be a farmer; even his laugh spoke of the finest temple education and breeding.

Khaliut laughed. "Thank you for the honor, Nekhti, but I am a simple farmer unaccustomed to such gestures."

"Excuse me, Sir. You do not speak like a farmer, but a nobleman."

"Truly?" Khaliut said, raising his brows.

"My Nekhti believes everyone not from our village is noble-born," said her father. Nekhti lowered her eyelashes. "There was one nobleman in our lineage. What was his name?" He scratched his head. "Ah, no matter."

Nekhti forced a pleasant expression on her face, because Khaliut had not taken his eyes from her.

Khaliut returned his attention to his host. "Your mention of nobility brings me back to the reason for my visit..."

Four

Maatre Kashta, King of Cush, walked out of the castle, with his thin, muscular arms behind him. A dull ache pulsated between his eyes. He took long strides up a flight of stairs to an expansive courtyard, his favorite place to think. The courtyard contained two stone benches, lush greenery, and a colorful garden; it also offered a picturesque view of Napata, the imperial capital. With imposing pink hills and limestone cliffs that stopped short of the Nile, the rocky desert was dotted with palm groves and sycamore trees. The king sat and ran a hand across his bald head. Placing his forehead in his palms, he massaged his temples with his thumbs, unaware that he had been followed.

First stopping at the foot of the stairs, the prince looked up, wondering whether he should proceed. Piye climbed the stairs and went to sit next to his father. Kashta raised his head and gave his oldest son a tense smile.

"I have received a letter from Kham." Kashta stood and clasped his hands behind him and paced. "Rumor has it that King Osorkon has taken an aggressive stance toward Cushites in Kham. He fears unification." Piye remained expressionless. "Is this hearsay? Posturing from a monarch uneasy in a land not of his fathers making? And should Cush care?"

Piye uttered not a word. He watched his father pace about.

The Sudanese monarch lifted his eyes and scanned the sandstone landscape. He turned to face his oldest son and looked into the young man's sharp brown eyes. "Yes, Cush cares."

Slowly, Piye smiled.

Waset

The reed boat bore no standard, sparked no curiosity, the kind of vessel seen everyday along the Nile River. When the courier disembarked dressed in a loin-cloth; he draped a stiff white kilt around his waist. The Cushite slipped on a gold armband, covering the tattoo on his arm that identified his position in Napata. Given Osorkon's latest decree against Cushites, the less attention he attracted; the better.

He set off toward Nobleman's Way, and wondered at the Royal Hawk's command. *Why now? Was some calamity soon to befall?*

***

Khensa placed the scrolls on the floor. "Yahweh?" She rose from the couch and gazed out the window, hoping to see a glimpse of the God who had performed such wonders. *This is astonishing. Though I have heard bits of this narrative as a child, I could never imagine the God of the Hebrews to be as powerful as this. This God requires no assistance. He needs no consort. How extraordinary!*

The body servant's soft voice sounded behind her. "My lady, a courier has arrived for you."

Khensa turned to see the servant stand aside. A young Cushite stood in the doorway. Khensa's hand flew to her mouth. The youngster did not cross the threshold. Khensa felt a fluttering in her stomach. *Why? After all these summers...*

The courier bowed in greeting. "His Majesty, King Kashta of Cush wishes your exile to end. You are to return home at once." He bowed and backed out of the door.

Khensa, Princess of Cush collapsed on the couch in tears.

***

Ten sunrises later found Princess Khensa gazing up at the blue-black statue of Amon-Ra. The statue had a golden kilt and headdress painted on, its left foot forward. Khensa had wandered down the corridors in the temple complex at Karnak, waiting for the servants to finish loading her belongings on a boat, thus beginning her journey home.

The princess turned toward the sound of clicking sandals against the limestone floor. She bowed her head in front of the statue, pretending to beseech the god for safe travel home. From the corner of her eye, she saw a priest, dressed in a long, white kilt, come around the corner.

"Your Grace."

Khensa lifted her head.

"Here are those annals my scribe copied for you." Khensa took the papyrus sheets and scanned the first page. The priest stared, incredulous. "An intriguing story. I think, that the ancients may have exaggerated, do you not agree?"

"No. I believe these accounts to be precise."

"Your Grace, you have raised me with your son. Are you now to say that you admire the God of former slaves?"

"I admire His power."

"Yes, but Amon-Ra."

"Amon-Ra has never done anything like this, Sen-nefer. I bid you good day. Life, health, and prosperity," Khensa said, turning away.

"Your Grace," he whispered. "A favor I beg of you."
He looked about the corridor, then handed her a small papyrus sheet. "Could you deliver this note to the king?"
Khensa paused, turned, and took the letter. She flipped it
over and noted the lack of seal. "The future of Kham de-
pends upon it," he said in a whisper. Khensa looked into
his earnest, black eyes. Even his dimples appeared to be in
motion.

"I certainly shall."

The priest bowed to her. He exhaled his relief. "Your
Grace, I bid you a safe journey." He watched her turn the
corner. When he heard footsteps at the corridor's end, Sen-
nefer, Third Prophet of Amon, bowed in front of his god.
He remained there until the armed guards, Pamiu's agents,
walked past him.

***

Meanwhile in Napata, Khaliut entered the royal palace
dressed in his finest linen tunic. He was escorted into the
smallest audience room where he waited for his father,
Prince Piye. The priest, Ay, had used his temple connections to gain Khaliut this audience.

When Piye entered the room, he took his time looking
over his son. "You are my oldest, though your brother
Shabataka, now holds that position due to your mother's
departure. Are you displeased?"

"No, Sir."

The king looked into his son's eyes. Khaliut willed
himself to stand still. His father's eyes could make a pillar
shiver. "You have no desire to ascend the throne?"

"I do not, Sir, though if I were so obliged, I would
surely do my duty."

"Well said." Piye moved to his seat, an ebony chair with carved panther faces on each arm, and sat. "How do you occupy yourself?"

"I am a farmer, Sir."

Piye gazed his son's smooth hands. "What do you really do?"

"I gather information for the Wasetian clerics."

"To what end?"

"To further their aims for the restoration of Kham, and to establish a Great House, preferably of native blood."

"Do you agree with this agenda?"

"I do indeed, Sir. The clergy has sent me to ask whether Cush would assist."

"No." Piye paused. "Why does Osorkon fear Napata's rise? Are his defenses so poor that he should feel secure if Ta-Seti remains weak? And what if the Two Lands unite under one crown, why is he concerned with the notion now? If you can provide accurate answers to these questions, then your career as a royal reporter may be of use. Good day to you, Khaliut of Waset."

Khaliut bowed and backed out of the room. *So Osorkon fears a strong Napata? A unified Two Lands? Father wishes to know why, as I do. If I can gather this information for Father, I shall flourish as a royal reporter and gain his approval all at once. I had thought his acknowledgment would suffice. But nay. I am his oldest son, he has admitted that much; it is not wrong to want more. What son would not?*

Neferua knows. But who provides her with information, other than her drunken father at the dining table? True, Ay had the influence to grant me an audience with my father, and there is no saying how much is overheard and passed about in the temples; but this is specific.

*And I must not forget the fair-skinned lad. Learning
who he is, and why he is in Cush, may prove fruitful.*

***

The next day, Khaliut pursued the clergy's request to
start a family. He had no doubt Katep, Second Propet of
Amon wanted him married to a royal relation for his ambitions if nothing else. Khaliut and Nekhti walked past a
field filled with grazing sheep. She wanted to walk in the
other direction, closer to the village, so she could be seen
by her neighbors.

It is not every day a girl is courted by a nobleman. *I
believe my Khaliut is bashful, the way he avoids people.*
She turned to offer her betrothed a smile.

Khaliut smiled; then placed a hand behind her elbow.
"Should I announce my intent to take you to wife?"

"Oh, yes, Khaliut, do." Nekhti grinned widely as they
turned and headed back toward the village. She sobered.
Her father had arranged for Nekhti to marry a *sem*-priest in
Meroe, but the lad's father withdrew the offer, probably
owing to Ay's recent demotion. She braced herself before
voicing the question heavy on her heart.

"Khaliut, where will we live?" Here in the village?"

Khaliut stared down at her for a moment. "Would you
like that? To live here in the village near your friends and
family?"

"No, Sir."

Khaliut laughed. "Where would you like to live?"

"In Napata." She lowered her lashes.

"Then we shall live in Napata."

Nekhti clapped her hands together; then skipped before
Khaliut. She could not wait to tell her family. She would
be a noblewoman. *And once Khaliut enters the royal capi-*

tal, he will start mingling with his class. And not mine.
Forget that farming nonsense. I shall encourage him to go
to court. We can live close to the palace. I mean, really,
with his speech and mannerisms, the royals will have to
hire him for something. Ambassador. Yes, that is it. He can be an ambassador
to an important nation. I shall be the wife of an ambassa-
dor. Nekhti twirled around, imagining herself among dignitaries from other nations. *I am Nekhti, wife of the*
ambassador from Cush, Khaliut. Friend of the Queen
Mother, Kasaqua, and friend of Queen Pebatjma...
"Nekhti." She stopped twirling. "This is your home, is
it not?"
"Oh, yes, Sir." Her cheeks grew hot. *By the gods, I*
nearly twirled past my home. With a sheepish grin, Nekhti
followed her soon to be husband inside. He took a seat at
the dining table, waiting for refreshment. Nekhti wandered
toward the back to see whether wine was available.

Kerit-Amon grabbed her daughter's ear and pulled her
outside. Nekhti clenched her teeth to keep from crying; she
knew if she did her mother would tighten her grip. "What is
the meaning of this? You fancy yourself marrying this
man?"

"Father has given his permission, Mother."

Kerit-Amon tightened her grip on the ear. "I know he
has, your father would give *you* anything. That is not what
I want to know. What have you done?"

"Done? Mother, I do not know what you mean."

"What have you done to get that man to marry you so
quickly? Are you with child?"

"No, I am not with child. Please, mother let go. I did
not do anything. He said that his eye took pleasure on me
for some time."

"Some time?" Kerit-Amon let go of her daughter's ear, because her fingers were starting to hurt. "That man has not been here long enough to eye you for *some time*. What have you done?"

"Nothing. Have I ever been accused of forward behavior?"

"No, of course not. This quick betrothal has made me suspicious. Why you? Why not Neferua, she is much more beautiful."

"She is too young, Mother."

"Right." Kerit-Amon paced around the courtyard, talking aloud. "You cannot marry your intended now that your father has lost his status. And if he is a nobleman that would ease Neferua into a better alliance..." She paused then strode back inside.

Nekhti went to the acacia tree and sat. Her mother came back outside and marched straight to Nekhti. Nekhti stood.

"When your wedding night is over, you shall ask your husband whether he has a brother for your sister. I do not believe for one moment that he is nobility, as you insist, but he is the best thing that has come through this village."

"Yes, Mother."

"I prefer a High Priest for your sister, but... just make certain, Nekhti, that he has a higher station than your Khaliut. Neferua is too pretty to be a farmer's wife." Nekhti remained silent. Her mother turned and went back inside but called across her shoulder. "Quit your loitering, Nekhti. Go to your wedding chest and see what is needed."

Nekhti ran inside.

"I suppose you think you are special because you are to marry first?"

Nekhti started. She was kneeling over her wedding chest, sifting through the bed linens she had sewn; some were half complete. "Neferua, you startled me, I did not hear your approach. Please come in."

Neferua remained standing in the doorway, with an indifferent look on her face.

"Surely, you are not angry because I am to wed, I am the oldest."

"Hmm. Only by two summers. If Mother had her way, I would be married before you."

"If Mother had her way, you would be queen." Neferua laughed. Nekhti winced. She hated her sister's laugh; she did not show hilarity often, but when she did, it sounded so...menacing. Nekhti had trouble imagining her baby sister as sweet.

"I was supposed to marry the high priest, you remember?" Neferua said.

Nekhti was surprised that Neferua shared this information with her, since they rarely spoke. Neferua confided in their mother only. "No, I did not know. I do remember father mentioning the high priest favored a woman from Napata, a close royal cousin."

"He did not prefer that sow! No one in high standing wished to be associated with the drunk."

"Who?"

"Father!"

"Oh, yes. I see," Nekhti said. She hated when Neferua and Mother referred to father in such mean terms. She knew their words hurt his feelings; Nekhti could see it in his eyes. Though she knew Father had a problem, she never made any references to it for fear of causing him pain.

"You are so simple, Nekhti. Now you are to be a farmer's wife, how appropriate."

"Do you think him just a farmer, Neferua? He speaks so well."

Neferua eyed her sister for a moment before admitting, "No, I do not think he was born to it. He chose it for some odd reason." They paused. Nekhti enjoyed having a conversation with her sister, and she did not wish it to end. "Mother says that I am to ask Khaliut for a brother for you."

Neferua's eyes grew stormy. "I care not for any of your references." She turned away. "Mother!"

Nekhti drew in a deep breath and steadied herself for the punishment soon to come.

Five

Prince Piye flicked his hand toward the seat opposite him, where Khensa, his sister-wife, sat. Piye took in her cinnamon skin and high cheekbones, features she had inherited from their mother. Her eyes were softer than her siblings, but direct. Khensa wore a braided wig and had barely any kohl on her eyelids.

"Who has reared my son? Schooled him in the ways of Amon-Ra?"

"The priesthood and scribes at Karnak." Khensa looked up at him. Piye's eyes bore into hers. He seemed annoyed, she could tell. What her punishment was to be, he gave no clue.

"Why did you not return after Shabataka's birth?"

"I did return for King Alara's burial, Brother. The atmosphere was too strained between your chief wife and me. I spoke with Mother and she agreed that I should return to Waset."

"You believed my firstborn would come to harm? Under my eyes, Khensa? You know that threats made against the royal brethren are a serious offense. Have you any proof of these allegations?"

"No, Sir. The only witness save me was a body servant who has retired from service."

"How convenient," he said. Khensa could not tell whether he was serious, or being sarcastic. Someone rapped on the doorframe. "Enter."

The chief royal aide entered. "Sir," he bowed.

Piye rose. Khensa waited until he quit the room before leaving.

***

The royal women sat in Khensa's chambers, watching
the servants unpack the rest of her belongings. *I am the
one who does not wish to be at home. Nay, that is not so. I
missed Mother and Grandmother Kasaqua.*

*They remain supportive of my decision. One day I have
hopes of visiting Jerusalem. I should like to see the earthly
realm that Yahweh calls home.*

The princesses' chattering grew animated, forcing
Khensa to return her attention to the present. She turned to
the younger princesses bearing linens woven in Kham.
"These are for the three of you." They squealed in delight.

"You all sound like hyenas," said Princess Tabiry,
Piye's chief wife stood in the doorway. "May I come in?"

"Of course."

Tabiry walked in and gave Khensa's possessions a
wide-eyed glance. She stopped and fingered a cotton coverlet stitched with running lions. "I cannot imagine what
you were doing in Kham so long."

"Can you not?" Khensa said. Her mother, Pebatjma,
gave her a small pinch in the leg.

"No. Dreadful people. Libyans and other former
slaves." She pretended to shudder. "With whom did you
associate? Was there anyone of your status?"

"There were the daughters of the nobility, of course.
The oldest daughter of General Purem and I were great
friends. Then there is Shepenwepet, the god's wife. I had
enough good company, I assure you."

Tabiry yawned. "And where is your son?"

"In Meroe."

"Doing what?"

"He is looking at property there, perhaps to farm."

Tabiry laughed out loud.

"Farming is an honorable profession, Tabiry," Pebatjma said. "Without it we would not eat, and I know that concerns you."

"Yes, I suppose it does, but a son of my husband. A great-grandson of King Alara, working as a farmer? How amusing."

"He is not the first to live below his station," Khensa said.

"Yes, I know about those distant relatives on the outskirts of society. But your son is a prince. What is his name? And how many summers old is he?"

"I prefer rather not to say."

Tabiry looked affronted. "And why ever not?"

"I just don't. Can we leave it at that?"

Tabiry glanced at the other women, who did not look up to meet her gaze. Only Pebatjma and Kasaqua watched the chief wife. "Very well, then." Tabiry left the room.

The women turned sympathetic eyes to Khensa. She tried to ignore them and resumed unpacking. Her focus fell on some papyrus sheets. She grasped them, then held them as gingerly as she had held her son when she left Napata, sixteen summers ago.

***

Ahouri, High Priest at Gebel Barkal in Napata breathed heaves, trying to keep pace with his cousin, Kashta. The king could tell by the older man's silence that he felt nervous. Crickets sang as the two made their way across dirt roads toward the southern sanctuary. The comfortable winter evening would soon give way to cooler temperatures.

Kashta tightened his cape around his shoulders and walked faster.

"Wait, Cousin," Ahouri said, panting. The priest made fists with his hands, then opened them again. He had done this several times since they left Cush, another reason that Kashta knew he was nervous.

"Sorry." The king's fleet had docked at Abu Simbel; the rock-hewn temple concealed two ships filled with bowmen. A smaller, unadorned vessel had transported them into Waset. The king and high priest waited deliberately for the long shadows of evening to appear in the city.

They arrived at the temple where nine bald clergymen greeted them. Three were draped in leopard skins; others were bare-chested and wore linen kilts. King Kashta stood out in his sand- colored kilt, matching cape, and skullcap. His fingers and wrists were adorned in gold. His eyelids sparkled with gold dust.

The priests bowed in unison. "Greetings, Your Majesty." The temple guards closed the door behind them. The priests escorted Ahouri and Kashta past a series of stone rams. Through engraved lotus columns, they entered a dim room.

In the corner stood a tiny golden statue of Amon, carved in the likeness of a man, his arms across his chest. Several incense burners were lit; Kashta knew the room would soon be filled with the cloying fragrance. Chairs were placed in a half arc in the room's center, with two high-backed chairs on the left end, where Ahouri and Kashta were seated.

The group settled and Kashta's thoughts turned to home and his pregnant wife, Pebatjma.

The Second Prophet, Katep, interrupted him. "Welcome, Your Majesty. Thank you for responding to our summons." Katep nodded at Ahouri. "And welcome, fellow

keeper of Amon." He strolled to the middle of the room.
His linen cape covered his sandaled feet. "King Kashta,
Ahouri tells me that you now have three strong sons." The
priest smiled at the king.

Glancing around the room, Kashta realized all eyes were
serious and resting on him. His eyes brightened and his
lips parted into a half-smile.

"I do, Piye, Shabaka and Miamon," he said, thinking, *the
priest should never smile, he resembles a panther.* The
ebony-skinned priest's eyes and forehead were forsaken,
shrunk behind a protruding nose and lips.

"Good. And daughters?"

"Yes, Amonirdes." The king kept his eyes on the priest,
following him as he strolled around the room, toying with a
huge ram head pectoral.

Kashta sighed inwardly. "Prophet, I am a servant of
Amon-Ra as devoted as you. Speak freely." From the corner of his eye, Kashta peered at Ahouri for a clue, but the
priest stared at the floor with his hands in balled fists.

"My apologies, Your Majesty, I did not mean to be vague." He paused before adding, "May I be blunt?"

"If you wish."

Katep grinned as if he were about to pounce. "Your
achievements, and those of your late brother King Alara,
have contributed to the southland. However, control of
Kham is still in the hands of the Libyans. And let us not
forget the petty lords in the delta, they are not without ambition."

"What do you propose, Prophet?"

"We, the clergy, would like the Princess Amonirdes to
succeed Osorkon's daughter as divine spouse to the god."
Kashta sensed the room tense. His cousin's body stiffened

with anticipation. "As you know, that act alone will
strengthen your claim to the double crown."

"And what qualifies me more than King Osorkon for the
double crown?"

Katep raised both arms in the air. "You are the Royal
Hawk, a descendant of Cush, and a lover of Amon-Ra.
Cush and Kham are brethren, despite our differences in the
past; Ham was our father. The lands of Ham are the home
of our customs, and our gods, and they shall remain so," he
said, pounding a fist into his palm.

"Tell me, Your Majesty, who is King Osorkon? What
are his claims of birth that make him a ruler? Is he a Khamite? Or a Cushite?" Katep peered at the king content at
the passion he saw stirring in the ruler's eyes.

"Those are excellent questions, Prophet. Lately, I have
been asking the same." He looked down at his cousin.
Ahouri's hands were at ease, resting on his thighs.

"I have another question, Prophet. Why would a priest
of your high rank support any woman as wife to the god?
Surely, you are aware that this office limits the clergy's
power."

Katep bowed, acknowledging the king's astuteness, then
smiled.

***

The nomination had gone well. The vote had been un-
animous. Still, Takeloth smelled a stench as foul as the final day of inundation. Why would the Wasetian clerics
vote in a Cushite princess to succeed Shepenwepet?

And why did Shepenwepet recommend Amonirdes to
succeed her? Did it have anything to do with the letter?
Was Cush conspiring against Kham? He had questioned all
the scribes, but none knew who had penned the letter to

Cush. Takeloth wondered whether they would tell him if they did know.

As a Libyan, his family, the dynasty of his fathers, was not popular. Nevertheless, it is a Libyan in power; his father Osorkon heads the Great House. Takeloth would not see a Cushite princess hold such a high office.

***

Amonirdes, daughter of King Kashta, stood in the castle's foyer weeping. Her belongings were packed and one of her father's best ships waited at the harbor to transport her to Karnak in Waset. The princess would be trained to succeed Osorkon's daughter as the next wife to the god. She had never expected such fortune, and would have been content to marry a royal brother and bear children. Instead, she would spend the rest of her life chaste and in service at the temple.

Amonirdes' brother, Piye, came forward and whispered something in her ear, which made her smile. He had such a dry humor. His face would seem oh, so serious, then he would say something funny. She would miss him, but he had promised to visit her in Waset.

Behind Piye stood Tabiry, his chief wife and the daughter of King Alara and Queen Kasaqua. Piye's other wives came forward; Abar, Peksater and Nefrukekashta approached, applauding Amonirdes' good fortune,

"What an honor, dear sister," Peksater said embracing Amonirdes. Both women were the daughters of Kashta, his queen, Pebajtma, and full-blooded sisters to Piye.

Khensa stood off to the side, closer to the king and queen. She felt a stranger, having spent the past sixteen summers living in Waset. She took comfort knowing that no one blamed her for fleeing. She had every right to pro-

tect her child. Was Tabiry jealous that Khensa had borne a
son before she did? No one, not even Queen Kasaqua,
doubted that Tabiry could be so spiteful. However, there
was no proof now, save for Khensa's own words.

Khensa watched Tabiry through narrowed eyes. *Well,
now that she has attained her goal of chief wife, the rest of
the family can live in peace. Oh, how she tormented us all.
And felt it her right to do so, after all she is the daughter of
the great king Alara. So? Are we not all relations by blood
to Alara?*

***

In Tanis, King Osorkon sat in the palace's audience
chamber on the golden stool that was his throne. Dressed
in a fringed kilt and golden sandals, the king's tanned face
was set in a frown. Heavy black kohl framed his light
brown eyes, and he wore the skullcap common among Libyan and Cushite rulers.

Pamiu sat opposite his king, his fingers drumming
against a bare knee. Heavily adorned in gold jewelry, the
Grand Vizier wore a vulture god pectoral around his neck.

Takeloth's booming laughter caused the king to turn his
attention to his son. "I believe that your men shall be for-
given this trespass. Their actions were for the well-being
of the nation. I do hope that they did not cause that letter
carrier too much grief."

"He shall recover, Sir," said Ankh-Osorkon, the Deputy
Vizier.

"Of course he shall. That letter was an outright invita-
tion for the barbaric Cushite hordes to intervene in Kham's
affairs. What will they try next?" Takeloth said, looking to
his father.

The king did not seem amused. "You mean, what have
they done?"

"Father?"

"I was referring to the Wasetians' latest move," said the king. "It seems there has been a successor to your sister, Shepenwepet."

"Father, do not worry on that score. The matter has not been settled. The clergy voted the princess Amonirdes in as the next First Wife of Amon," Takeloth said to Pamiu.

"Yes, I know."

"Why, yes of course you would. But I have not approved the choice."

"You have not approved? When was I to learn about this?"

"After I completed my investigation, Father. The letter to Cush vied for my attention."

"May I remind your majesty that the position of First Wife is significant," Ankh-Osorkon said. "A most serious political move indeed it lays the ground for legitimacy to the double crown." His brows creased in worry.

"I need no reminder of the fact, Deputy Vizier," the king said. A recent move had brought the ancient office of god's wife back to prominence, bringing the constant infighting among the king's relations in the Wasetian clergy to an end. "Send a courier to Napata, informing the High Priest at Gebel Barkal that I have not approved the motion for the Princess to succeed my daughter, nor will I.

"Father, Shepenwepet named Amonirdes as her successor," Takeloth said.

The king's face reddened.

"Your Majesty, the princess has arrived in Karnak this day," Pamiu said.

Takeloth interrupted. "Do not worry, Father. I have placed her in custody."

Pamiu's head whipped toward the High Priest. Ankh-Osorkon slapped his forehead with his hand.

"You have detained a woman of royal birth?" the king said.

"Temporary arrangement, Father, I assure you. I need more time to investigate the source of her nomination. The princess shall want for nothing. Every luxury will be at her dispersal until the time for her safe return to Napata."

"Takeloth, My Majesty has no quarrel with the Great House of Cush. Nor do I wish to start one."

"I understand, Father…"

"Resolve this matter at once," the king said.

***

The moment Pamiu returned to Karnak, he scheduled interviews with every scribe. He stood behind a large cedar desk, tapping it lightly with a reed pen. "So," he said to the scribe standing before him, "there was nothing out of the norm that took place during this time?"

The scribe pursed his lips. "Umm…" He shook his head. "No. Nothing." He looked thoughtful, then put a finger in the air. "Except when Princess Khensa requested copies of the reign of Thutmosis the Third."

Pamiu let the pen drop on the desk. "What for?"

"I know not, Sir."

"When was this?"

"Shortly before her departure to Napata."

"Who copied the annals for her?"

"I did, Sir." The scribe looked down at his feet.

"Did you deliver these annals to her?"

The scribe looked up, his eyes bright. "I did not. The Third Prophet did. Shall I fetch him for you?"

"At once," Pamiu said. The scribe scurried out of the Vizier's office.

A short, stocky priest with a boyish face entered the room. "You are Sen-nefer, Third Prophet of Amon?" Pamiu came from around his desk and stood in front of the priest.

"Yes, Vizier. I am at your service," he said, bowing.

"What did you give the princess, Khensa?"

"The reign of Thutmosis the Third during the Hebrews' departure from Kham."

"Do you know why she had this portion of history copied?"

"Yes, Sir. The princess was fascinated by the wonders performed by the God of the Hebrews."

"This is my final question to you, Sen-nefer. I suggest that you think before you answer." Pamiu paused, and watched Sen-nefer.

The priest drew himself up and nodded his head.

"Did you deliver any other correspondence to Princess Khensa that day?"

"Yes."

"What was it?"

"I know not. It was sealed."

"Who gave it to you to deliver to Princess Khensa?"

Sen-nefer smiled. "Vizier, I believe that you are all out of questions."

The Vizier speared the priest with his eyes.

"Katep, Sir. The Second Prophet."

Pamiu went back behind his desk. You may go in peace, Sen-nefer."

Sen-nefer bowed. "Sir." He walked out calmly. Once outside, he ran back to the temple quarters.

***

Katep stared into the flickering candlelight. He lifted his goblet and drained the remaining wine. He always had wine before bed; it helped him sleep soundly.

Ignoring the spent candle, Katep rose and headed for his couch. The moment he closed his eyes, he heard a rustling sound near the door, then hurried footsteps departing.

Katep rose and knelt by the door, where a papyrus sheet lay. He took it to the table and placed the sheet close to the candle.

A short note. Hieroglyphs drawn in haste. Enough, though, to get the priest moving.

A line of torch lights moved through Waset's deserted streets. Soldiers marched up the avenue at Karnak, past the stone rams that lined the walkway and up to the temple's entrance. The head officer banged on the door. "Open! In the name of King Osorkon."

A scribe opened the door slightly and peeked out. He saw the red and white head cloth on the first officer. "May I help you?"

"We have orders for the arrest of Katep, Second Prophet of Amon-Ra."

"The prophet is not here Sir," the scribe said, opening the door wider.

"We will see," said the officer.

"As you wish."

***

In Napata, during the last month of winter, two Wasetian clergymen were ushered into the audience room where King Kashta sat on his throne, a golden seat with lion paws for feet. Katep and Sen-nefer approached the king and bowed.

"Our gratitude to the Great House in Cush," Katep said.

"Welcome, gentlemen. My family and I wish to thank you for the concern shown toward my daughter. Please, have a seat," Kashta motioned them toward chairs.

"Greetings, men," Katep said to the princes and advisers. They responded in kind, and the priest took a seat facing the king.

"Have you the note, Priest? Proof that my daughter is in custody?" Kashta said.

"I am afraid that I have not, Your Majesty. I set the note to flames before leaving Karnak. I did not wish to indict my informant. However, the content was clear. King Osorkon had ordered the apprehension of my staff and me, and the continued detainment of Princess Amonirdes."

"Have you any indication as to why Osorkon would want to incarcerate my daughter?"

"I believe, Sir. that it is owing to the nomination of Amonirdes as the heiress to Shepenwepet. My sources tell me that neither the High Priest nor Osorkon favor a Cushite occupying such a high office."

"And do you believe your information to be precise?"

"Yes, Your Majesty. I trust my contact implicitly," Katep said.

Kashta fell silent. He stared at the priest for a moment, then raised his eyes to his staff.

That evening, when the castle quieted Kashta made his way to his wife's apartment. He stood at the room's entrance watching her weave. Pebatjma sat erect working at her loom. A square table next nearby with small bowl filled with her favorite evening drink - warm goat's milk laced with honey. A carved Lebanese wood couch set behind her, its large, deep red pillows stuffed with goose feathers. A female's room. Kashta, though king, was bound by culture and custom to remain outside it.

"What worries you?" Pebatjma said without looking up. Kashta made a guttural noise that, Pebatjma knew, meant he would forego convention.

He entered the room, lifted a high-backed chair from its place in the corner, and sat across from his queen. "If Osorkon wishes to monitor Cushites in Kham, it is his concern, is it not? Especially if no Cushites are harmed. Why go a-warring? And if I start a war, would the lads see fit to finish it?"

"They will finish it if you say so. Nonetheless, you have started it when you sent our Amonirdes to Karnak." He grunted his assent. "Piye and Shabaka hold you in high esteem. If you leave word that this war will be fought to victory, they will do so."

"Truth. A strong Cush and an unstable Kham would never do. But for the squabbling dynasts in the Delta! Who in Horus' name knows how many rulers they have there now? Every Libyan and his goat has been crowned king." Pebatjma laughed softly.

"Kham has allowed them far too much power: the clergy should have never given the Libyans so much leave; wresting it from them will be difficult." Kashta fell silent. Pebatjma looked up from her loom and watched him.

"Does the cost of this war equal the reason? If Osorkon removes Amonirdes from her position, she can come home straight and marry Miamon. And we shall leave Kham to the Khamites." Pebatjma smiled, relieved. "For now."

Six

Nekhti crossed her legs and sat. She loved to come on the rooftop at this time to watch the colors that appeared when Ra slipped down in the sky. Not to mention that the roof was the ideal place to hide when she wanted to avoid Mother and Neferua.

Father comes up here often, probably for the same reason as I. I am to marry. She smiled to herself. *Everyone is so jealous, Neferua especially, though I doubt she would ever admit it. My friends all think that he is a nobleman; he must have spent much time in court.*

Nekhti focused on the sun's descent. *Does anyone save the palace astrologers pay mind to the sunset as I do? It always goes down, but it never looks like it is moving, at least not from here. Orange, yellow and lavender. By the gods, that is clever to make such a beautiful spectacle in the evening. It is as if Someone is saying, "you see, all is well. Do not worry. Trust me."*

But is it Amon-Ra? Or Someone superior to him? I wonder if there is a hierarchy of gods, that we know nothing about. Father, though a priest, has never mentioned it. Strange. But if there is a hierarchy, and there is Someone greater than Amon-Ra, then this God must be the one who paints the skies.

Nekhti brought her knees up to her chest. "Who are you? Are you Amon-Ra?"

"No, it is I, your father," Ay said.

Nekhti laughed. "Evening, Father. I did not hear you come up the stairs."

"Because," he said, sitting next to her, "you were so busy talking to the sky."

"I love to watch Ra's descent."

"Hmm. As do I."

Nekhti paused. "I was wondering whether there was Someone greater than Amon-Ra? I mean, look how beautiful this is."

Ay leaned in and whispered. "Honestly, daughter I do not know." He put a finger to his lips.

"Silence on that score."

"Why do you serve at the temple so faithfully?"

"Your mother is determined to see us distinguished. And the priesthood is an honorable profession." He shrugged. "I do not care for it." He sighed. "I get the distinct impression that it is all a waste of time. But enough of the dreary talk; what about your forming a household? Are you not excited? A life partner of your own, children?"

"Yes, Father, I am excited."

"And," he said, poking her in the shoulder. "You get to escape this house." They laughed together. "Fortunate are you, Nekhti."

"What do you think of Khaliut? Do you think he is of noble birth?"

"Nekhti, that is unimportant. I know you will not believe it. When you are older, you will see that people are the same, despite their rank and fortune."

"Does that mean no, you do not think so?"

"He has been reared with privilege. That I do not doubt. As for the details, I do not know. He is mysterious, do you not think so?"

"Indeed. I like that about him."

"What does he say of his parents, his siblings?"

"Only that his father lives in Cush somewhere, but he has never met him. And his mother is from Kham, and he was raised there. He made no mention of his siblings, though mother is pushing me to ask him for Neferua's sake."

"Hmm. Extraordinary." Ay creased his brows.

Nekhti looked up at her father. "What is it, Father?"

He smiled, but said nothing. "I must be off." He stood. "Remember, if you discover that Amon-Ra has a superior, you must tell me straight away. That would be my excuse for quitting the priesthood."

"I shall, I promise."

"Ay! What are you saying there? Did I hear mention of your quitting the priesthood?" Kerit-Amon yelled from the bottom of the stairs.

Ay turned and gave his daughter a conspiratorial wink. "Nothing, Dear. I was speaking of someone else," he said, going downstairs.

The official announcement of betrothal between Khaliut and Nekhti was made; Ay traveled to Meroe and registered the union at the main temple. When he returned home, Sissi and her family had arrived bearing gifts for the new couple.

Sissi looped an arm through her friend's and led her away from the other guests. She whispered into Nekhti's ear. "You have your prince."

"A nobleman, I am sure."

Sissi sobered. "The union made by your parents, was it the intended who broke it off?"

"Yes owing to my father's demotion."

"And your sister Neferua's reputation."

"Reputation? Of what do you speak, Sissi?"

"Activities, better said." Sissi looked around them before saying. "You shall know soon enough."

***

Nekhti's bottom felt aflame. They had been traveling since before dawn, hours straight without a break. The two-hundred mile journey was an endless golden canvas across the Bayuda desert, dozens of low hills covered with date palms. A while back they had encountered tribesmen dressed in loincloths, with colorful tattoos on their arms and wearing ivory necklaces.

Nekhti had thought they were nearing Napata, because there were people around, but they continued behind the same caravan with which they had started. The wagon in front of them was full of screeching monkeys. There were no other women in the caravan, and her new husband was often lost in his thoughts.

Nekhti turned to Khaliut, but before she could ask, he answered for her. "Not long now, hold on, we are almost there."

Nekhti smiled, adjusted her bottom on the seat and turned her thoughts to their new home. She was not hoping for anything fancy, not right now at least. Two rooms, one with a large central living area. Firm stairs would lead up to the roof, where she could entertain on the warmest evenings.

A spacious storeroom underground where perishables could be kept cool. The kitchen would be in the courtyard or downstairs. It would be big enough to fit a three-sided brick oven for bread baking. Later, when Khaliut accepted his position in the Great House, Nekhti would get some ivory chairs and benches for the main room.

Yes, that would do nicely. She stretched her neck to see whether she could glimpse the city. *Oh, I cannot wait to arrive.*

Nekhti clapped her hands when they approached barley fields. She knew they would soon enter town at the upper end of the Dongola Reach. She spotted an open field, where large horses were trained for chariots. As they entered town, Nekhti greeted passersby. Heading deeper into the city, Nekhti looked for more people to meet, but everyone seemed distracted.

"Khaliut?" she started, as a company of soldiers jogged past.

"Yes, I wonder what is going on." Khaliut's eyes scanned the scene before him. He brought the wagon to a stop. More troops armed with copper blades, spears, and shields, were coming toward their wagon. Nekhti followed them with her eyes as they passed; then she saw the warships in the harbor.

"We are at war," Khaliut said, tightening his grip on the reins.

"But with whom? Not Kham surely?"

Khaliut looked around for someone to ask. Another company of men approached, all with heavily muscled arms. Khaliut knew they were the bow troops, Cush's specialty. An officer followed the troops.

"Excuse me, Sir. My wife and I have just arrived. Can you tell us what has happened?"

The officer eyed Khaliut hard for a moment, as if he knew him. "The king has declared war on Osorkon the Third for placing our Princess Amonirdes in custody."

Khaliut looked at Nekhti. Her eyes grew wide. "I see," he said, returning his attention to the officer. "Thank you, Sir."

The officer gave a curt nod and continued his way.

"We are at war," Nekhti said breathlessly.

Khaliut started the wagon again. The glitter of regalia caught his eye. "Look, Nekhti. Down by the harbor."

Nekhti rose to see where he was pointing. Chariots. Royal chariots formed a line, their occupants watching the loading of men and supplies on the ships. She felt a thrill course through her. "The royal family? Is that the king?"

He replied in a whisper. "Yes, can you see the Royal Hawk on the chariot door, there?"

"Oh, yes, I can." Nekhti stared at the man in the center. King Kashta was bare-chested, and stood with his arms folded. He had medium-brown skin and a snub nose. Instead of a crown, he wore a skullcap. And the horses, Nekhti had never seen such large horses, and with plumes at that. "Wait, Khaliut. Who are they?"

Khaliut started to answer, when a fair-skinned with a boyish face caught his attention. The lad was speaking to a royal guard. Khaliut pointed to the tall prince to the king's right. "That is the Crown Prince Piye to the king's right," he said. The wagon made a sharp left. "Next to him is Prince Shabaka, then Prince Miamon." Nekhti wanted to know more, maybe to stop and get out and greet the royals, but Khaliut urged the team away at a fast clip.

He too was awed by the royal sighting, so why does he not stop so we can meet them?

Close to sundown, Nekhti stood in the middle of a one-room hut, gawking in disbelief. This was where her husband, her nobleman, had left her. He traded the oxen they had received for a wedding present, for the first hut he came to. He brought in the heaviest items from the wagon, kissed her on the nose and left.

What kind of husband is he? I have never heard of such a thing. And where was he in a hurry to go? Surely, he was not thinking of fighting in Kashta's militia.

Nekhti went outside to gather the last of her household items. She ignored the neighbors' curious looks at her belongings, including the wedding gifts from the High Priest and his wife back in Meroe. She uncovered a large faience vase, wiped it down with a cloth, and gingerly carried it inside. She heard awed murmurs from the village women. They probably never saw such finery before.

Once the door was shut, though, Nekhti sank against the mud brick wall and cried.

After an evening of darting through taverns, sleeping inns, and temples, searching for him, Khaliut found the lad at sunrise, making his way down the harbor. He seemed the same age as Khaliut, but shorter. *Was not this man in the temple at Meroe with Neferua? I am sure of it.*

To the Cushite sailors and harbor workers, seeing a foreigner down at the harbor was nothing to concern them. However, it meant something to Khaliut, but he waited until the man came closer before speaking in Aramaic. "Dark hair and eyes are common in these parts. Fair skin, however, is not. What brings you to Napata, my friend?"

The lad laughed. "Where else could a young man like me purchase a fine horse?"

Khaliut's mind raced to trace the man's accent. "Have they no prime horseflesh in Damascus?"

A faraway look came into the man's eyes. "Ah, Damascus the wondrous jewel in Syria... I do not know. I have never been there. I heard that the finest steeds were to be had right here on the Dongola Reach. What about you, Sir? What brings you to Cush?"

Khaliut chuckled. "Why, I am a Cushite."

"Ah, well, that makes sense. I will be on my way now, Sir."

"Good day to you. Have a safe journey back to Jerusalem," Khaliut said with a smile. The young man laughed aloud but continued to walk away. He kept his pace leisurely, in case Khaliut's eyes were still on him. He turned slightly and saw that Khaliut had taken his seat in a boat.

The lad had been at the harbor since dawn, and he knew in whose boat Khaliut sat. He found the ship's captain talking to a military officer nearby, and waited patiently until the officer had finished listing his instructions to the ship's captain. When the captain turned toward the lad, he had a frown on his face.

"My good captain. A word of caution if I may," the lad said, in broken Khamitic.

The captain looked the man over before answering, "Yes."

"There is a Khamite man on board your vessel, Sir. I have good reason to believe that he is not a friend to Cush, and that he was in your capital to obtain information."

The captain used a hand to shield his eyes and squinted. Indeed, the lanky fellow with the long head, short straight nose, and chestnut complexion did seem Khamitic. "What makes you so sure?"

"I spoke to him moments before addressing you. His conversation was painfully vague, and given the current political situation, he gave me every reason to suspect."

"Gratitude. I'll see to it."

"Safe journeys to you."

Khaliut watched the captain come toward him. He climbed ashore and strolled away. Scowling, he determined to track down Neferua. Khaliut boarded a boat headed toward Meroe; though filled to capacity, the captain dared not refuse passage to the tall man with fierce eyes.

Back at the temple where they first met, Khaliut watched her come forward. She had a sway to her hips, that she had not had the first time they met. Was this for him? His face was covered, as it was the first time they had met. Does she know who he is? "What word do you have for me?"

She smiled seductively.

"This is no game, Madam."

She walked around him. "What would Osorkon give to save his crown? Who would lend their support if hostilities erupted?"

"Your fair-skinned friend, whom you meet in this temple, from what part of the world does he hail?"

Neferua's hand moved toward her chest, where she kept a concealed blade. Khaliut grabbed her wrist and held tight. "Do you sell secrets to anyone who pays, Madam? If so, you compromise Cush and Kham. Tell no more intelligence to foreigners, else you be accused of treason. Now, from where does this lad hail?"

"Jerusalem," she spat, her body trembling with anger.

Khaliut turned and walked away. *And to Jerusalem I go...*

Seven

Judah

New towers had been built in Jerusalem, at the Corner Gate. More towers had been erected in the desert, and new wells had been dug. New shields, spears, helmets, body armor, bows and slings were issued to the army, priority given to the mighty men of valor, the army's twenty-six hundred chief officers.

Judah, King Uzziah's little desert kingdom, had grown strong.

"...and proud," Azariah, the priest, said. He glanced at Jeiel for support, but the scribe stared straight ahead. Azariah spoke about the king to the sole person who could speak reason to him, his mother.

Jecholiah turned from her weaving to give the priest a hard look.

"I do not mean to be critical, Your Grace, but his majesty's strength grows daily."

"As does Judah's," Jecholiah said.

"Yes, that is so. Though lately, the king's speech and manners have reflected his achievements."

"Are you prophesying a fall for my son, Azariah?"

"No, Your Grace, I was hoping that you might encourage him to look on his success as Yahweh's favor."

Fearing the direction this conversation was going, Jecholiah did not answer.

"Preferably before the Almighty Himself sees fit to remind him," Azariah said. Again, Jecholiah made no response. Azariah bowed quickly and left. Perspiration had formed on Jeiel's brow. He wiped it away, gave a hurried bow and followed the priest out.

Jecholiah stared at the door for a few moments. Then she rose, snatched her shawl off the chair, and headed for the king's quarters.

Jecholiah stood in the doorway of the king's throne room. Inside, her grandson, Prince Jotham, sat in a winged chair reading a scroll. His father, Uzziah, was also reading as he walked around the seat that was his throne. *Or is he strutting?* Jecholiah watched in silence, trying to assess her son's attitude. *Was Azariah correct? Has my son grown proud? Cocky?*

She tapped on the door. Uzziah looked up, his brows creased in annoyance. When he saw who it was, his face broke into a smile. "Mother, do come in."

Prince Jotham rose and greeted his grandmother with a kiss on the cheek, then led her to a nearby couch.

"I am reading a congratulatory letter from Syria on our recent developments," the king said. "We are no longer a petty desert kingdom, Mother. Look." He picked up more scrolls off his throne, each bearing a signature stamp from a foreign nation. "My fame has spread to other countries. We have not been this revered since King David's time."

"True, Son. I trust that your newfound fame will not cause your heart to be lifted up."

"My heart lifted?" Uzziah cocked his head. "Where did you get that notion?"

"The priest, Azariah, came to speak to me." She told him all that the high priest had said.

Uzziah barked a laugh. "The priesthood was all smiles when I humbled the Philistines, then the Arabians at Gur Baal, and they had nothing to say when I subdued the Meu-

nites. But now, my heart is lifted. Tell me, Mother, did the
priest have a prophecy against me?"

"No, Son."

"So this was not a word from the Lord, but the priest's.
If the Lord was displeased, why did He not say as much?"
He raised a hand to stop his mother from speaking. "Do
not worry, Mother. I shall thank Azariah for his watch
over my soul, but I am the anointed ruler of Judah. I have
Yahweh's permission and authority to reign, is that not
so?"

Jecholiah wrung her hands together.

"Mother?"

She breathed deeply. "Uzziah, the sons of Aaron are also anointed by God. They are called to be priests. Azariah
would be remiss in his duties, had he not called attention to
where attention was due."

Uzziah sneered. Jecholiah arched her brow. Jotham
opened his mouth, surprised. When the king saw his mother's expression, he sobered.

"My apologies, Mother. The absurdity, though, of a
priest having more authority than the king."

"Son, it is not a question of authority, but accountability."

"Hmm…" Uzziah said, tapping the tip of his nose with
the scroll. "Accountability. I am capable of being everything to the people of Judah. The Commander-in-Chief of
the Army, Judge, Intercessor, and if necessary, Priest."

Jecholiah's eyes widened in alarm. She turned and met
her grandson's startled expression.

Uzziah raised his hand, signifying that he had heard
enough. "If you will excuse me, Mother, I have correspondence to attend to."

Jecholiah bowed to her son and left. Once she was alone in the corridor, she prayed. "Lord God, God of my ancestors, Abraham, Isaac, and Jacob, please do not allow my son's pride to harm him, or to cause hardship for the people of Judah. If he raises himself too high, Lord, I beseech You for the sake of his eternal soul, take him down."

Uzziah looked up from his reading. A tall person, his face shielded by a long cloak passed the doorway. Secure within himself, the king watched, unalarmed. Hananiah, a captain in King Uzziah's army appeared in the doorway, he watched the person slip out of the palace.

"Captain? Come in," Uzziah said. "Tell me, what is going on in Mizraim? I have heard conflicting reports." He raised the scrolls for emphasis.

Hananiah paused before turning to address his king. He bowed and said, "King Kashta of Cush has declared war against Mizraim."

"What trespass has Osorkon committed against Kashta?"

"King Osorkon remains king, though there are three other leaders reigning in the country, Peft-something in Nennesut, Nimlot in Khemenu and Tefnakte in the western delta. Princess Amonirdes, Kashta's daughter, has been placed in custody."

"I had thought Osorkon a smarter man than that, much more sensible than his predecessors. Continue."

"The cult of Amon-Ra at Waset has conspired to place the princess as chief spouse."

Uzziah wrinkled his nose. "A wife to their god?"

"Indeed, Sir." The captain allowed himself a smirk before continuing. "Her detainment was an action taken by Osorkon's son, Takeloth III, High Priest of Amon-Ra. Someone had informed King Kashta that his daughter was imprisoned, which was not entirely true."

"The clergy's words?"

"No. They claimed to not have known of the incarceration; however, it is thought that this same source alerted the Second Prophet, Katep, to flee Waset."

"Captain, I need more reliable information from Mizraim. I received an earlier report declaring that the delta monarchs have invaded the south. The Wasetian clergy would prefer a Hamite in power, yes?"

"Yes, Sir. A return to their ancient traditions."

"Send someone to Cush and Mizraim."

"I have. But there is reason to question his loyalty..."

Uzziah arched a brow. He slowly sat on his throne. "Do tell."

***

Nekhti had no food. She could no longer ignore the aromas of fresh-baked barley bread and lentil stew coming from neighboring homes. The village had quieted. The children had been called in for the evening meal. Her neighbors had given her gifts of food to welcome her arrival, but she had eaten the last of it this morning.

Nekhti had bartered her least liked wedding gifts for household items: A bed, a panther skin rug, two lamps with wicks, and yards of quality linen. She had bought these items for their real home, not this hut. She thought Khaliut would have returned by now.

She peeked out of the window matting to see if anyone was about. Good, everyone was inside. She grabbed her water bucket and a woven basket then hurried outside to the well. *Should I pen a letter to Father and ask him to retrieve me? No. How scandalous. I cannot go home. I cannot bring that manner of disgrace on the family. We are still reeling from Father's demotion. Father would re-*

port Khaliut to the authorities, accusing him of abandonment. And rightly so.

Mother would wish to know exactly what I had done to scare my husband off so soon. Nothing, I would say, but she would never believe it.

Nekhti gathered mimosa and tamarisk wood for fuel. She picked dates and olives from the trees right outside the village, then filled her bucket with water from the well. She took a long last look around the village. Men were leading their oxen in for the day, but none was her husband. He had not returned. Sighing, she turned back toward home.

"Evening, Nekhti," said Merit, her closest neighbor. She dipped her bucket into the well.

"And a good evening to you, Merit." Nekhti tried to walk away at a pace that would not seem rude.

"Have you gotten all settled in? I did not smell your evening meal. I do know how long it takes to set up a household," Merit said. She turned to Nekhti, lowering her voice. "Would you care to join us for a meal?"

"You are kind. But I have eaten some cucumbers and bread, and am full." Nekhti patted her stomach for effect.

Merit smiled. "Good. I would not wish for my newest neighbor to be hungry."

"I am not." They returned to their homes in silence. When Nekhti reached her front door, Merit placed a hand on her arm.

"You know, Nekhti, you may consider selling at market."

"At market? Why, I am no merchant. I am the natural daughter of a second prophet. I have no experience in such a thing."

"But surely your mother taught you how to weave? Flax grows aplenty near the river," Nekhti lifted her chin. "Or you can mix cosmetics items, pomades, oils, and creams."

Nekhti thought of the aloe-based ointment she had made for her mother's dry, cracked skin. Maybe her mother needed her to return home. She smiled. "A worthy suggestion, Merit. I am grateful for your thoughtfulness, but my husband said before he took leave on business, that we would be living here temporarily. When he returns, we shall be moving closer to the palace. He is a nobleman, you know."

"Yes, child. You mentioned it as so. Nevertheless, if you need anything, do not hesitate to make it known."

"I am grateful." Nekhti entered her hut. Once inside she collapsed against the door, glad her stomach had waited until now to grumble.

The following dawn, Nekhti left her home carrying her largest basket. She ignored the greetings from the fishermen and farmers heading to work, and engrossed herself in locating the flax and other plant items growing nearby.

She had had a restless night. The hunger pangs subsided for a time, but came back when she awoke. She had decided not to go home in defeat. She would sell at market until she could move out of this wretched village. If anyone said anything, she would say that she was a widow. Her husband had left on a business trip, and was eaten by wild animals. *How just was that!*

And if Khaliut did return, she would inform him their marriage was over, and he could return to wherever he came from. Her next household, she would make sure the man was noble born.

How she was to do that she had not yet thought out. He would be a priest at a nice-sized temple; she would never suffer this humiliation again.

After filling her basket with aloe and flax, Nekhti headed home. She raised her chin when she entered the village proper, in case her neighbor Merit was about. *I did not smell your evening meal! What did she do, stick her head out of the window and sniff around my courtyard?*

Well, she can smell my meal this evening. I shall make haste and prepare Mother's favorite ointments, sell them at market, and have a feast for one.

***

Jerusalem

Jecholiah did not intend to eavesdrop, but from her window overlooking the palace courtyard, she could hear almost every word. Her son, King Uzziah, was speaking in harsh tones to Azariah, the priest. Jecholiah willed herself to be still, wishing her heart would beat softer. Was Uzziah confronting the priest about his conversation with her?

Does the king have the right to reprimand the Lord's anointed? The queen mother hoped that her son did not go too far. Perhaps he would come to his senses and see how high his heart had risen.

It quieted for a moment. Then Azariah spoke, but his voice did not boom through stone walls like Uzziah's did. The long pause in the conversation diverted the matriarch's attention. The Salt Sea seemed motionless from where she sat. In the distance, sheep grazed on rocky hillsides.

Jecholiah lit a footed lamp on her windowsill, then brought a chair and sat to watch the sun dip below the horizon. Priests walked toward Jerusalem's main temple. Je-

choliah counted at least eighty men standing in front of the
sanctuary, all looking toward the palace.

"Who are you to speak to me in this manner?" the king
said.

"I am a priest of the Lord Most High," Azariah said in a
loud voice, his patience wearing thin.   A son of Aaron.
Please, Your Majesty, it was merely an exhortation. I did
not mean to start an argument."

"Listen, Azariah, son of Aaron. I am the king of Judah,
also anointed by the Lord our God. My rule is known
throughout the world, I will not be rebuked by a priest."

Jecholiah grabbed the windowsill with both hands.

"Your Majesty, I beseech you to pay heed. You have
become strong, yes. And in the eyes of the world you are a
mighty king. But you and I both know that you have
reached this level of fame because you diligently sought the
Lord. Do not let your heart be fooled into thinking that it
was owing to your strength. Give God the glory, is all I ask
of you."

"Azariah, whether the Lord God is displeased with
me, He can make that clear to me Himself. Until He does,
as His chosen king, I shall do what I want, and when I
want."

Jecholiah gasped. When she heard the quick clicking
of sandals she stood. Her son descended the palace steps
two at a time, and headed toward the temple.

"Lord God, I pray for your mercy…" Jecholiah said.

Uzziah sprinted up the temple stairs and banged into
the sanctuary. Azariah and all eighty priests ran in after
him. Uzziah looked about, then grabbed a censer and
moved to the incense altar.

Azariah stuck out his arm in front of the king. "Your
Majesty, it is not for you to burn incense to the Lord, but

for the priesthood, the sons of Aaron. Please leave the sanctuary. You shall have no honor from the Lord our God."

Uzziah's face reddened. He glared at the priest for a moment. Then loud intakes of breath were heard among the priests. The priesthood took a collective step back away from the king. Uzziah's hand with the censer went limp. "What? What is the matter?"

"King Uzziah, a spot of leprosy has broken out on your forehead," Azariah said. "You must leave the temple, for you are unclean."

Uzziah reached up to touch his forehead. "My Lord and God," he said. Letting the censer fall to the ground, the king collapsed to his knees.

Azariah turned to the priest on his right. "Go and find an isolated house fit for our king to spend the remainder of his days. Then fetch Prince Jotham; he must now preside over the king's house and judge the people of Judah."

Azariah returned his attention to his monarch. The leprosy had now covered his entire face and was moving down his neck. The king began sobbing. Was his sorrow owing to true repentance or the loss of his royal power?

Azariah did not know.

Eight

At the royal palace in Napata, Princess Tabiry entered the women's dining hall, where she joined the heated debate already in progress. "Absurd. Why should the Great House in Cush make war with Kham?" The royal women sat around the dining table. A servant entered and set a platter of honey-roasted fowl with glazed dates on the table.

"Tabiry, war is not our primary concern, but the safe return of our beloved Amonirdes," Queen Pebatjma said.

"And do you think, that Cush's entire navy is necessary to rescue her," Tabiry said. A servant held out an ivory chair for her.

"The men do not know what strength awaits them in Kham," Pebatjma said. "Perhaps they think it is best to be well prepared." The queen creased her brows. "Do you have no concern for our beloved, Tabiry?"

"Why, of course I do. That dreadful high priest Takeloth should be relieved from duty, his name removed from every obelisk in Kham." A collective gasp sounded.

"If Amonirdes comes to no harm, surely there is no need to erase the man's name from the afterlife. That is severe, Tabiry," Pebatjma said.

Khensa, who had remained silent during the debate, spoke up. "Do you think the rescue of Amonirdes is the brethren's sole objective, Pebatjma?"

"I do not see any other reason to make war. What say you, Kasaqua?"

The Chief Wife of the late king Alara looked thoughtful before speaking. "I believe there remains discontent over the Libyans' power in Kham."

"Why should it be any of our business who rules the Great House in Kham?" Tabiry said. "As long as the former slaves do not turn their ambitions southward."

"Your discussion is conducted with such passion, that we have decided to join in," said a male voice. King Kashta entered the room followed by the royal brethren, Piye, Shabaka and Miamon. The servants gaped for a moment at the men's appearance in the women's area, then rushed to get more food. Kashta took a seat at the head of the table.

"Our objective is twofold. First, we shall tend to the well-being of our Amonirdes. Second, we shall oblige the heart of Kham, its priesthood, and nobles, by helping the Black Land return to its ancient traditions." He directed a pointed look at his niece, Tabiry.

Tabiry's eyes glittered with distaste. She popped a date into her mouth and chewed slowly.

"And how long do you think this campaign should last, my lord?" Pebatjma said to Kashta.

"One full summer."

"We are expending all of this energy for only Waset?" Tabiry said.

Kashta waited until the servant had filled his goblet with palm wine before answering. "Waset is the seat of power in Kham. Once we have the south, in truth we have Kham."

***

Waset had not yet awakened. Few people were up at this hour, except the fishermen and farmers who wanted to get their day's work started before the sun rose.

At the riverbank, Khaliut sat underneath a sycamore tree, wrapped in a woolen blanket. He watched Cush's naval fleet inch into the harbor. Kashta's golden barge had two chariots with plumed horses on board.

Nothing to be found in Jerusalem. No lad, no intelligence as to why Osorkon fears reunification. If I continue working for the Wasetians, and further their aims to restore power to southern Kham, and indeed the clergy, would Father approve? Tis' my best hope.

His response to my assignment was vague, though he did wish to know Osorkon's motives. That should be my aim until another assignment comes to me, if another assignment is given.

Khaliut sat up straight. *The lost letter. If Pamiu retrieved it, then it is certain the king has seen it. What was said in that letter? Katep, the Second Prophet wanted it found at once. Perhaps the letter hinted at treason. But why blame Cush? Why persecute Cushites in Kham?*

The dew on the ground seeped into his coverlet. As the ships drew nearer, Khaliut could see tall warriors standing on board, armed with spears and sickle swords. When the darkness faded and the day dawned, people began gathering at the river. Women paused en route to the market. Noblemen stopped their chariots to stare. Boys en route to temple school gaped in awe.

Khaliut stood. He slipped away and boarded a vessel heading toward Tanis.

***

Ahouri, High Priest at Gebel Barkal, followed Takeloth through the columned hallways of Karnak. At the end of one hallway, Princess Amonirdes stood between two temple women. Ahouri approached, bowed, then mur-

mured soothing words. He gave a brief, cursory examina-
tion of her person before leading the way out of Karnak,
and toward her father.

***

Deputy Vizier Ankh-Osorkon ran toward the king's
chambers, his sandals causing enough commotion to waken
the palace staff. He pounded on the king's bedroom door.
"Your Highness, arise. It is most urgent." He waited a few
moments and pounded again. "Your Highness, arise."
Seconds later, a bedraggled king opened the door, glaring
unimpressed at his deputy.
    The Deputy Vizier bowed. "Sir, King Kashta has ar-
rived…"

King Osorkon had bathed, dressed, and was breaking
fast in one of the palace's many gardens. He looked up
from his bowl of steaming barley porridge with dates to see
that the Deputy Vizier had returned. Deputy Ankh-
Osorkon bowed before his king.
    "Princess Amonirdes?" Osorkon said.
    "A courier from Waset brought news. Vizier Pamiu
and High Priest Takeloth have seen to her release, as you
requested."
    "Good. Kashta will find this rumor of his daughter's
detainment groundless. A woman who spends the day
weaving in a luxurious apartment at Karnak is hardly imprisoned. Who has told the king otherwise? The Wasetian
clergy is my guess. But Kashta and princess Amonirdes
will return to Napata, and all this unpleasantness will
cease."
    Ankh-Osorkon waited until the king swallowed some
porridge. "And what if Kashta wants more?"

"More? Deputy, King Kashta will get his daughter and nothing else." He resumed eating.

***

Nekhti heard a familiar snicker. She whirled around and faced her sister. "So the noble class lives in this manner?" Neferua raised a brow at her older sister's simple frock, then she allowed her eyes to wander toward the meager selection of cosmetics on top a wooden stool.

"Good day, Neferua. What brings you to Napata?" Nekhti refused to oblige her sister's humor; this was hardly amusing. Selling like a common merchant was the last thing she thought to be doing.

"Khaliut is away on business." Nekhti swept her hand across her goods. "This keeps me occupied while he is away."

Neferua threw her head back and laughed.

Nekhti watched the tears stream down Neferua's face, as she struggled to catch her breath. She turned away from her as a young woman approached and stopped in front of Nekhti's wares.

Nekhti picked up a small clay cup filled with aloe paste. "Your mosquito bites will heal faster with this," she said pointing to the tiny swollen marks on the girl's arms.

"Truly?" She offered a loaf of emmer bread. "Will this do?"

"Yes." Nekhti made the exchange and thanked the girl. She turned back to her sister. "Are you done?" Neferua had left. Nekhti peered through the sparse crowd of vendors, but she could not see where Neferua had gone.

***

Two Cushite guards escorted Grand Vizier Pamiu off Kashta's ship. The Vizier did not look pleased as he hurried toward his chariot. People peppered him with questions.

"Are we at war?"

"What is Cush doing here? And what have you done to the Princess?"

"What has the Great House gotten us into?"

Pamiu ignored the queries and climbed into his chariot.

***

The afternoon Pamiu arrived in Tanis, Takeloth was already there speaking with his father. The king looked up at the Grand Vizier's announcement. "Grand Vizier, we have everything under control, yes? Good. Takeloth has gifts that he will take to Kashta with our regrets over this misunderstanding."

"I am afraid, Your Majesty, that it will not be as simple as that."

"Why not?"

"King Kashta did not just come for his daughter. He came for Waset."

A chariot bearing the standard of King Osorkon moved through Tanis' narrow streets. "What are our chances of withstanding Kashta? Surely, the delta lords can help."

"The Deputy Vizier is summoning volunteers from every delta district. I have done the same in Waset. I have sent couriers to each district informing them to assemble the able-bodied males," Pamiu said.

Osorkon sighed. "I am getting too old for this."

"May I suggest a co-regent sir?"

"Grand Vizier, I may not have a throne at Ra's descent."

"I doubt that Kashta would reside in the south, Your Majesty. We could negotiate a treaty that allows you to remain in power in the delta."

The king stared out at the reed marshes. "I have a deep love for the Two Lands, Vizier, as I am sure you do. I would give my crown to avoid a bloody war. My dynasty alone has caused Kham enough trouble. I would like a peaceful resolution to this, Grand Vizier, see to it."

"I will, Sir."

However, five sunrises later, an unusual standoff was under way in Waset. On the Nile's western bank, king Osorkon's royal charioteers waited in battle formation. Behind them were the royal advisors who resided in Waset. The Cushite army had taken position on the Nile's eastern bank. The bow-troops stood at attention in front of Kashta's ships, and waited for war.

Also on the river were the curious, who sat in papyrus boats and skiffs, eyeing both armies. Several Wasetian nobles sailed their ships down the Nile right among the warring factions, as if it were a typical day in the first month of summer.

The impending hostilities took on a festive atmosphere. A young woman played a lute, much to the delight of the onlookers, some of whom danced. Bets were waged on who would win the fight, Osorkon or Kashta. Vendors hawked everything from honey-glazed dates to mortuary guides. In case a loved one lost his life during the skirmish, a guidebook to aid his way in the afterlife could be bought in advance.

The House of Rejoicing, a brilliant white palace located on the Nile's west bank, had been built for Amenhotep III.

During the ninth year of his reign, the king commissioned
the palace on a site that stretched for thirty thousand square
meters. The palace had separate apartments, a library, audience halls, kitchens, storerooms, sprawling gardens, and
festival halls. The administrative offices, the same ones
used by Amenhotep III were now the space where Osorkon's southern-based staff worked.

The mud brick palace still bore the legacy of Amenhotep
III and his chief wife, Queen Tiy, whose cartouches, oval
drawings with knotted ends containing the names of the
royal pair, were painted throughout the interior. When the
royal parties met in the audience room, Kashta was struck
by the notion that Osorkon had chosen to meet here for a
reason.

Indeed, as a show of power, Osorkon climbed the small
steps leading onto the platform where the throne sat. The
move did not go unnoticed by Kashta and his entourage,
but the Cushite ruler waited until Osorkon was seated. The
Libyan nodded his assent for the king of Cush to make
himself comfortable.

Pamiu stood in the room's center and read Kashta's
terms.

"You ask much for a misunderstanding, Sir," Osorkon
said to Kashta.

"True. But reigning in Waset will give me satisfaction.
The opportunity to rebuild its past, restore her temples, and
give Kham back her proper heritage."

A heavy pause fell on the room.

"I will not give in to your demands, King Kashta,
noble as they are. Waset will fight."

Kashta stood. "As you will. When will your troops be
ready to engage us? Sunrise?"

Deputy Vizier Ankh-Osorkon gaped at the Cushite king. Osorkon exchanged an odd glance with his son Takeloth. Not sure of what his response should be, the king nodded.

Kashta was correct in his belief that Osorkon chose this palace to meet for a particular reason. As he walked from the audience room toward the king's chambers, the walls were decorated with bound captives, foreigners, being made an example of by the king of Kham. When a foreigner walked these corridors, they were to feel trampled underfoot.

Kashta felt nothing of the sort. He paid Osorkon's subtle message no heed. As far as he was concerned, the Libyan was the foreigner, not he.

***

Neferua moved the through the dusty streets, dressed in a simple linen frock, with a cloak shielding her face. She slithered through Kham's armed forces like a desert snake. Not too far ahead, she spotted her friend, the fair-skinned lad. Dressed more conservative this day, he wore a loincloth and a leopard-skin cloak, and stood close to the Wasetian clergy.

Neferua's confident stride slowed when Khaliut came around a pillar, his body toward the lad is face looking in Neferua's direction.

She cursed.

Khaliut moved toward the lad, his long legs eating the desert ground. The lad sensed danger. He ducked and moved between the priests toward the river. Khaliut being taller could keep pace.

Once the lad cleared the group of clergyman, he ran. Khaliut sprinted after him. A ship in the harbor had pushed away from the shore; the lad ran and leaped in, urging the occupant to sail, now. Khaliut neared him and was about to follow, when he slammed into a body.

"Khaliut, let him be."

A harried Khaliut faced the Third Prophet, Sen-nefer. "What! Why? Who is he reporting to?"

"A message has been sent to Jerusalem about him. Let the Hebrews do with him as they wish. He is no concern of ours."

"Neferua said he was Hebrew, but I have doubts. What would a tiny kingdom like Judah care about Kham?"

"I agree," Sen-nefer said, lowering his voice he added. "If I must take a guess, it would be Ninevah whose interest is satisfied." Khaliut raised his brows in question. Sen-nefer made a sweeping gesture with his arms. "Who else would care whether Napata rises? And the Two Lands become one?"

Nine

Khaliut hummed as he filled a wineskin with water. *Can Kham be restored? The needless civil wars fought by the Libyan dynasts were disheartening. In order to regain world power, there must be a return to the ancient traditions, and it must begin with the monarchy.*

And yes, I understand Katep and Sen-nefer are working toward this end. But who else? And whether truth is spoken, I suspect the priests are more concerned with clergy's restoration of power, than anything else.

Out of this a most fortunate circumstance had arisen. Napata. Imagine Cush as the foremost power in the Nile Valley. With four rulers at present claiming authority in Kham, what were the chances of them putting aside their differences to fight Cush?

But if my royal grandfather grants me an assignment, I could gain Father's approval as a royal reporter. That would be all the better. I could stay at home more, with my Nekhti, though we must remain in Napata. She would be sorely disappointed if we cannot move as promised.

What shall I do? If I am to succeed as a reporter, I must remain discreet. If I am too visible, I shall be no use to the Great House.

Khaliut prepared to head home. He loaded a rented barge with the finest linens, linseed oil, a jug of wine, reed dishes, and a wooden bed, all for his new wife. Now, if he could just remember which village he had left her in.

***

Early morning light streamed through the palace windows. Khensa marveled at how quiet the palace was now that the men had departed. She would have liked to go with them to see her friends.

She sat alone in the dining hall, breaking fast with a plate of figs and cup of milk. *How does my Khaliut fare?* His last letter had been vague about his whereabouts. *But what good news he did reveal! He has taken a wife. I had feared he had no interest in setting up a household. I am happy he has proven otherwise. I cannot wait to meet her.*

"Are you in peace this day, Khensa?"

Khensa looked up to see Tabiry enter the hall. Piye's Chief Wife was dressed in a white ankle-length gown. Khensa schooled her features amiable. She had thought the household had finished eating, and she could dine alone. "Yes, thank you, Tabiry."

"I thought it best under the circumstances to speak things out," Tabiry said, coming to stand behind a chair opposite Khensa.

"What circumstances do you speak of?"

"The war. If Kashta does not return, my husband shall be the Royal Hawk. I would wish for you to feel at home here, though your conduct remains that of a stranger. I am aware that your son is the oldest, but my Shabataka shall follow his father in succession to the throne."

"I see."

"Good. Then you harbor no ill feelings toward Shabataka?"

"No, it is no fault of his that I fled to Waset."

Tabiry's eyes flashed. "Nor is it the fault of mine. I resent your implication that I have behaved indecently."

"I believe that you did. And I shall always believe so. Whether you admit it, is your affair."

Tabiry slammed her palm on the table. "My husband has ordered me to make peace with you Khensa. However, your attitude makes that difficult."

"If *our* husband asks me whether you have attempted peace, I shall tell him this conversation in full. But he also shall be made aware that we remain in disagreement about my departure."

Tabiry stalked out of the hall.

***

When Khaliut's boat arrived in Napata, five weeks later, the capital was celebrating victory in southern Kham. People sent gifts to one another. Newborn males were named Kashta. Tattoos and murals appeared on temple walls and obelisks, showing Osorkon kneeling before Kashta; someone even drew it on the palace wall in Tanis.

Kashta had achieved his objective; his united forces were the determining factor to his success. The political factions in Upper and Lower Kham prevented Osorkon from presenting a strong military response to Cush's invasion. He was, therefore, forced to sign a treaty giving the Cushite king dominion over Upper Kham.

Osorkon would remain king, but owing to his advanced years, his son Takeloth III would be co-regent. Princess Amonirdes was adopted as the successor to Osorkon's daughter, Shepenwepet, as divine spouse to Amon-Ra.

***

Khensa walked into the Thirsty Palm tavern and sat on a stool. At midmorning, the establishment had four customers. The man seated next to her had fallen asleep on his stool and was snoring loudly. The barmaid approached Khensa, taking a full moment to look at her. "Those are fine clothes you are wearing. Can I get you something to drink, my lady?"

"Pomegranate juice, please."

The barmaid's head jerked back as if she'd been slapped. "Juice?"

"Yes." The barmaid took another good look at Khensa before going away, muttering. A loud snort came from the man next to her. He slipped, almost falling off the stool as he awakened. Khensa watched him from the side of her eye. He straightened himself, then dozed off again.

"In peace, Mother?" Khensa turned to see her son.

"Yes, Khaliut. And you?"

"I am. How do things fare at the palace?" He took a seat on the stool next to hers.

"Better than I had expected. Tension remains between Tabiry and me."

"Does she remember why you left?"

"Yes." Khensa paused as the barmaid placed a clay cup filled with pomegranate juice in front of her.

"Anything for you, Sir?"

"Palm wine." The barmaid graced him with a huge smile before going away.

"Where is your wife? Shall I be meeting her soon?" Khensa said.

"Not now."

"Is she with child?"

"Not since last I saw her." Khaliut accepted the wine goblet with a smile.

"How did your father receive you?"

"Formally. His demeanor was difficult to read."

"Yes, it usually is. Your grandfather is not well. The injuries he suffered in the war are not healing."

"Will father co-reign?"

"I do not know. Will you stay close to Napata?"

"I cannot promise so. If there is a change in the political scene, especially if it interests Cush, I will be away. But worry not."

"Easier said." She looked down in her cup. Khaliut covered her hand in his. Khensa whispered. "May Yahweh be with you."

Khaliut's eyes widened.

***

Must every village look alike? Khaliut wondered. After retrieving his wagon and team, he had hired a youth to help him load the goods bought in Kham, then spent the last hour searching for his home. Villages in Kham had at least a banner or some indication of the town's deity. Khaliut strained his eyes, looking for a landmark, something he could recognize as the village where he'd left his wife.

Finally, he decided to stop at the next village and ask.

Minutes later, he came to a small village. At its entrance sat a few old men talking loudly and laughing. Khaliut stopped near them and addressed the man whose tattoo signified rank.

"Greetings, Sir. Can you tell me of Nekhti of Meroe?"

The elder stood to his feet. "Why you must be the nobleman from Kham?"

That woman talks too much. "Yes, Sir. I am Khaliut."

"Khaliut? The name sounds familiar...I am the village's elder. Was your business successful? It seems so." The man peered at the two cows hitched behind the wagon. "Those are fine looking livestock, Sir." The other men raised themselves, and inspected Khaliut's cows. After a brief discussion on the beasts' well-being, they looked to see what else Khaliut had in his wagon.

Khaliut followed their gazes. "Gifts for my wife."

"Of course," said the elder. "And well-deserved, I might add. You left your wife in a strange village, alone. Not a relative nearby. Why, if it was not for my wife, your Nekhti would have had a horrible time. 'Twas my wife, Merit, who suggested that your wife sell at market." The elder paused to wait for Khaliut's thanks, hopefully as a coin.

"Selling at market, is she? Good, Sir, I thank you for your family's goodwill," Khaliut said. He could find his home now that he knew that this was the right village. He turned the team around. "Good day to you, Sirs."

"Your Nekhti will not be at home, Sir. But if you should desire a meal, my Merit would be happy to attend to you. We are your closest neighbors." Khaliut nodded his thanks. The men bowed their farewells and watched the nobleman and his goods leave.

Khaliut had no trouble locating the elder's house, his family's totem, was painted outside. A woman peeked out of her door as Khaliut halted the team. Children began to gather around him as he disembarked. Khaliut patted one youngster on the head before opening his front door.

Khaliut unpacked the goods, led the livestock into a gated yard adjacent the house, then fed them. He was about to lie down on his mat when he heard a knock on the door.

"Greetings, Sir. I am Merit, your neighbor and the elder's wife."

"Good day, Madam. I met your husband this day."

"Your wife will not return from market until Ra's going down. May I present you with this basket of food to hold your appetite until her return?"

Khaliut took the basket. "Thank you, uh, one moment." He turned inside and returned with a linen handkerchief. "Please accept this gift as a token of my appreciation of the kindness you have shown my wife."

Merit bowed. With a wide grin, she accepted the expensive present from Kham, and excused herself.

Khaliut found a jar of wine and poured himself a cup. He removed the napkin from Merit's basket and took out dried fish and bread. When his stomach was full, Khaliut lied down and fell asleep.

Despite the holiday-like atmosphere, Nekhti managed to sell all her cosmetics this day. She had a bucket full of food, including a duck that she intended to fix for her supper. She had also bought yards of linen. She was going to make herself a new gown to wear to a party given at the royal palace, but she had to start tonight. Rumor had it that the king and his court were due back in Napata in two sunrises.

A grand celebration would be had on Kashta's return. *And I intend to be there. My dress will rival any noblewoman's. Even the queen's. One of those farmers, a few doors down has a son reported to have talent in designing tattoos. I will summon him to create me a portrait that would celebrate Cush's victory; one that the king and queen will surely notice.*

Nekhti's mood remained pleasant until she came to the village's entrance. Naked children ran about playing, and women gathered at the well to gossip. The normal scene in every village, from here to Kham no doubt, but Nekhti hated the commonness. Peasant farmers and fishermen. The place smelled like fish and cow dung, all day and night.

When did she come to despise the lower classes? *What a wretched being. I have become my mother's daughter. No one who lived in "this village" had any connection with the noble class.* How she longed for news from the royal palace. *Did the queen accompany Kashta to Kham?*

Nekhti wanted details, especially those about Waset's surrender. *No one in "this village" or at the market had any news.*

What did they talk about all day? The size of the fisherman's catch, or how high the Nile would rise. Who cares? Nekhti's livelihood as a cosmetic seller did not concern itself with such things. Her destiny as an ambassador's wife did not either.

Nekhti ignored evening greetings from the village's elder and strolled to her hut. Two little girls, twins, were running toward her. "Your husband is home. He has brought you presents. Fortunate are you, Nekhti of Meroe!"

Nekhti gave a brief smile at their last statement but said nothing. She quickened her pace. *I shall give that husband my mind, leaving me alone in this smelly village. What sort of mate is he?*

Mentally stoking her anger, Nekhti opened the door with force. Khaliut bolted, but seeing it was his wife, he flashed a smile. She gave him a fierce scowl in return. "Greetings, dear one," Khaliut said.

Nekhti slammed her purchases on the table.

"I have missed you," Khaliut said.

"How could you leave me for so long? What kind of husband are you? Negligent, that is the kind of husband you are, negligent," she said. Tears coursed down her cheeks.

"My dear, I told you before I departed that my business was most urgent, and that I had no idea how long it would take. I do apologize for any inconvenience that my absence caused you, and I intend to make it up to you. Starting now, look at the wonderful gifts I found for you," he said, pointing to a corner in the room where he had deposited her presents.

"I have had to sell at market to survive. You left me with no food..."

Khaliut looked aghast. "I am truly sorry, dear. It shall never happen again," He reached out to her.

Nekhti pulled back. "I had thought to marry a nobleman instead I am forced to sell like a common merchant."

"Nekhti, I have told you countless times that I am a farmer. We are commoners, and the sooner you learn to accept our status, the better."

"That does not mean that we have to live in this wretched village. When shall we leave?"

"Soon, my dear. For now, I have had a long journey and am tired. I will return to my rest, please wake me for the evening meal." Khaliut turned back to the bed and was snoring lightly in minutes. Nekhti had much more she wanted to say... and ask. She desperately wished to know when exactly was "soon."

After putting away her parcels, she took the duck outside to the kitchen to prepare for roasting. She was stoking the flame, when she heard an animal's moan. Nekhti moved cautiously toward the noise. *Are those cows? By the gods! We are rich. We shall have milk. What else did he buy?*

She went back inside to see the rest of her husband's purchases. She gazed in awe when she came across the linens. *These are Khamitic linens. Where did he get the means to purchase such? You silly goose. He is a noble-man's son, remember?*

Well, he has never said that he was, nor has he denied it altogether. But these items must have been bought in Kham. So that is where he went, maybe a family emergen-cy needed tending. But why not take me, his wife? Unless he is ashamed of me, after all, I am now the daughter of a Fourth Priest.

Near nobility in "this village," but closer as a peasant in a Khamitic noble house.

Nekhti put away her gifts, vowing not to use her linens until they moved. They were far too rich for this hut.

***

One morning, Ahouri, the High Priest came to pay a visit at the royal palace. He had come to talk sense to Kashta's Great Wife, Pebatjma. The king was stubborn; he knew his health would not improve, because the priests and palace physicians had told him so. Kashta would never recover enough to rule both Cush and Upper Kham.

The task belonged to a younger man namely Prince Piye. He is ready Ahouri intended to tell the queen. No one can doubt his maturity; the quiet, spiritual lad is as steady as the Nuba Mountains.

He excelled in his military training, leading a bow troop at fifteen summers. Yes, the crown prince is ready to take his father's place.

A servant escorted Ahouri to the sitting room. She bowed her excuses, promising the priest refreshment on her return, then went to fetch the queen. The priest knew that the royal hairdressers attended the women. The first thing a Hamitic woman of noble birth did shortly after waking was to summon the hairdresser.

The women were engrossed in the story of the feeble attempt by a nobleman to win the hand of Princess Merit-Amon. The women burst out laughing. Queen Pebatjma turned to see the servant awaiting her attention.

The servant returned. "The queen will meet you in the dining hall. The women have not broken fast yet; please follow me." She led the priest down a long corridor. Artwork etched on the walls portrayed the royal family and its court during the reign of King Alara.

They turned left and entered a huge dining hall. A solid limestone table sat in the center, hoisted by its fat, stone legs. Ivory vases filled with fresh lotus blossoms, lined the table's middle.

Ahouri stood behind a chair for a few minutes. Soon, Queen Pebatjma emerged, wearing a loose ankle-length dress and flat leather sandals. Like most Cushite women, her hair was cut close to the scalp. "Good day to you, High Priest," said the queen. "I am both honored and curious that you have chosen to speak with me, and not the king."

Ahouri bowed, smiling sheepishly. "Your Majesty."

Queen Kasaqua, wife of the late King Alara came in, followed by the princesses, Tabiry, Peksater, Khensa, Merit-Amon and Nefrukekashta. "Oh, I shall miss our Amonirdes. Did you read her last letter?" Kasaqua was saying.

"Yes," Khensa said. "So far away in Waset. Shall we visit her sometime, Mother?" she asked Queen Pebatjma.

"In time, dear. Let Amonirdes first get trained in her temple duties."

"She must have had such a scare being held by that horrible Takeloth," Tabiry said.

"Ladies," said Kasaqua. "The high priest has come to speak with our Pebatjma. Be silent and take your seats."

The young princesses bowed their heads. "Welcome, High Priest."

Ahouri, who had remained standing, bowed and was seated after the women were all comfortable. He faced Pebatjma. "Thank you, Your Majesty for receiving me. I have come to beseech you to reason with our great King Kashta."

"Uh-oh," Kasaqua said. The women snickered.

Ahouri smiled and continued. "His health reports are not favorable, and his duties and responsibilities have increased."

"What do you suggest, High Priest?" Pebatjma said.

"I suggest that the crown prince be allowed to co-reign with His Majesty." A long pause ensued as the ladies looked to one another.

"Do you think he is ready, High Priest?" Kasaqua said.

"Indeed, I do, Your Majesty. He is a solid, capable lad in both mind and body." Ahouri waited for a moment. Pebatjma's brows creased. Tabiry stared at Pebatjma, her mouth open slightly.

"I do not mean to cast doubt or fear into the Great House, but I must speak forthrightly. I do not think that our great king would make an impressive appearance at the next Sed Festival. His poor health is all too apparent, despite the recent victory in Waset."

The queens did not flinch. The princesses, however, all looked horrified.

Ahouri continued, "All that is needed is one bad inundation coupled with the king's poor health. If that occurs, whom will people blame? The king, of course, and we must endeavor to keep the dynasty strong and vibrant more now than ever." The servants came in with jugs of beer, and reed plates filled with goat cheese, roasted leeks, and cucumbers.

Pebatjma answered the priest. "Your words ring with reason and truth, as always, High Priest. I would hate to see my husband put to death because some farmer did not like his harvest. I will speak to Kashta this day," she said, looking around the table. Kasaqua nodded to Pebatjma her approval over the decision. "There now. Enjoy your meal High Priest; Cush will be well."

Ten

Nekhti added onions to the pot of chickpeas and stirred. She placed the lid on top of the pot and removed it from the fire. Sitting on a small granite bench, Nekhti picked at the hardened skin on her hand. She had stayed home from market again today; indeed, she had stopped going altogether after Khaliut's return.

Neferua was right. I should not be living like this. Fortunately, Neferua did not see where we live. By the gods! How embarrassing that would be.

To think I am the daughter of a priest and I live in this manner. True we have more cattle than any family in the village, not to mention better household items. Indeed, I have looked at my neighbors' things and noticed that my housewares are far superior.

Should I begin gathering our belongings? Khaliut has been home for some time now, surely he has found us better accommodations. He has not mentioned so, and I do hate to pester him.

Away from the fire, Nekhti grew chilled. She went inside to get a shawl, then headed out toward the small field that Khaliut farmed with earnest. The ground was still moist from the last inundation, which went well, so the village declared. The river had a reddish tinge to it from the muddy silt.

Soon every village garden would be green as tiny sprouts of cucumbers, leeks, beans and onions burst forth.

Nekhti watched her husband sprinkle steer manure across the soaked bare ground. She wrinkled her nose.

Why is he caring for the crop that way? Perhaps, when we sell this hut, a thriving vegetable garden will increase its value. Why, of course.

Khaliut straightened. "Cow dung not only makes fuel, but it will make our vegetables bigger and tastier."

Nekhti wrinkled her nose again. Khaliut laughed shortly. "Our garden never smelled this bad. Mother and Neferua would have said something." She sighed. "I do miss the news telling at our evening meals."

Khaliut came to attention. "What manner of news?"

"News about the royals, the going-ons among Napata's noble-born."

"Who was the supplier of this news?"

"Why, Father, of course. At times, Neferua has intriguing tidbits to share."

"And where did your father come about information?"

"I do not know." Nekhti lost interest in the conversation. "The meal is ready, but I suspect you will head to the river beforehand. To bathe."

Khaliut smiled. "Yes, of course."

"Khaliut, why do we care whether the vegetables are big and tasty, surely we will not be here at harvest time."

"We will, Nekhti."

"You said that we would move, do you not recall?"

"I said soon."

"Yes, but when is that? Khaliut, I am eager to get out of this village."

His eyes flashed. Nekhti knew this as a warning signal to back down. He pointed to the heap of dried cow dung. "Take in the fuel, Dear. I will be in shortly."

An hour later, Nekhti had dried her eyes and resigned herself to spending the rest of her life in this village. She sat with her back against the wall looking around her home, the mud-brick hut that she seemed destined to never leave. *I am Nekhti, wife of a peasant farmer. A farmer, who drinks palm wine, can read and write glyphs and hieratic, and compute figures.* "What are you thinking of?" Khaliut asked. He smelled a lot better, and had shaved again, a practice he learned from growing up in Kham, no doubt. She did not hear him come in.

"Nothing." She stood and went to set the table.

"Speak truthfully, Nekhti."

"I thought that perhaps you would consider adding another room to our home. In case I get with child. Or, my parents come to visit. Or, maybe your mother would consider traveling from Waset..."

"Nekhti, I am not opposed to expanding our home, though I doubt that your father could persuade your mother to pay us a visit. And my mother will never return to Cush."

I hate to lie to her, but the woman talks too freely. If mother visited, Nekhti would tell the entire village that her mother-in-law was noble born. People may not remember the name of the son, Princess Khensa left Napata to protect, but they will recognize her name, grand-daughter of the late king Alara. "But as you say, if you become pregnant..." He looked at her expectantly.

"I am not."

"Hmm," he said, disappointed. She placed a jug of pomegranate wine on the table. Her neighbors would be envious to know that her husband, the peasant farmer, had wine instead of beer at each meal. They would probably ask her how he could afford wine. She did not know.

Khaliut came behind her and placed his hands on her shoulders.

How does he do that? I never know when he approaches. He moves like a cat.

"Do not despair. We shall not be living here for the rest of our lives. I suspect by next summer, we should be ready to move, if not sooner."

"Truly?" Nekhti beamed.

***

From an upper balcony, Katep watched Kham's long-time enemies make their way in to Karnak's courtyard. The Sais delegation included Tefnakte and his Chief Counsel, Madanen. The delta lords had come to put their mark on the treaty, signifying their loyalty and recognition of King Kashta.

Another chariot pulled up outside the temple complex. The brother of King Osorkon, Bakenptah, General of Nennesut climbed out. Osorkon has already arrived with his son, High Priest Takeloth. Katep smiled as Takeloth passed. The High Priest had ordered Katep to be relieved of his priestly office, but Kashta had granted Katep a pardon.

I am not as disappointed as my peers may think. True, I wished to occupy the office of High Priest. Since the Libyans have been in power, that position has been awarded to the king's son. I had hoped that Kashta would forego this Libyan practice in favor of Kham.

Yet, he has not done so No, I am not very disappointed. My ambition has not wavered in the least. I will see the land of Ham return to her ancient and glorious traditions, with a strong, influential clergy and king, as in the days of old. And there are other ways to do that.

"Katep, Second Prophet of Amon," Tefnakte came to stand next to Katep, with a golden goblet of wine in his hand. "Greetings to you, Priest. Tell me, what do you get out of all of this?"

Katep had watched the delta lord walk toward him, though he did not think that the Libyan would dare speak to the man that had summoned Cush. But perhaps he did not know that.

Katep faced Tefnakte with a forced smile. "I get nothing, Lord Tefnakte. If Ma'at reigns in Kham, I am content."

The priest returned his attention to the delta dynasts and their entourages.

"Is the Great House of Cush without gratitude? After the service you rendered, I would think you'd promoted to High Priest." He did not look at the priest but pretended to study people below.

So he does know. What could he want? Surely he realizes that my ambitions are contrary to his. "You believe you are well acquainted with my aims, Lord Tefnakte?"

"Indeed," Tefnakte said, taking a sip of wine. "If we are both successful, you will be high Priest. I shall rule the Great House, and there shall be no more warring in the ruling dynasts. Ma'at shall be restored to Kham."

Katep gave a short bark of a laugh. "And you trust me to help you with this?"

"Why, yes. I know that you are on good terms with the Great House of Cush. Even you must realize that while they rule the Southland, your ambitions go no farther than this balcony."

Katep said nothing. When he turned to face Tefnakte, he said. "Speak to me of your plans, Lord Tefnakte."

740 BC
Jerusalem

Khaliut looked up at the descending sun, gauging how much time he had left. He stepped over a broken potter's wheel, and made his way through an olive grove. The aromas of roasted lamb and charred rosemary made his stomach grumble.

"What brings you to this little spot of the world, friend?" a male voice said behind him.

Khaliut stopped and turned around slowly. He knew that voice. "I have come to see the new cities being built," he said pointing eastward. "There in the Judean hills."

The lad looked to the east. "Ah, yes. Those cities will be a sight." He flushed red. "Uh, I am sorry about any inconveniences I caused you, especially in Napata. I hope I did not disrupt your travel plans."

"No. And you? What brings you so far from Ninevah?"

"Ah, Ninevah. The crown jewel crafted by my ancestors."

I knew it. Khaliut felt a rush of exaltation. *He is Assyrian.* "Your ancestors? Nimrod was a son of Cush. Twas my ancestors who built that crown jewel."

"Ah, well I suppose if you care for details. Come, my friend, let me buy you a beer."

"On the Sabbath eve in Jerusalem? No one will serve you a beer. I have those cities to see. And you, what does an Assyrian want to see in Judah?"

The lad turned to leave. He raised a finger in the air. "Assyria, my friend, likes to see everything." Khaliut watched him depart, then hurried to the gates before they

closed for the Sabbath. He needed to find an inn to bathe
and eat. A good night's sleep before tomorrow's meeting
would be ideal.

Stars filled the ink-black skies in Jerusalem. Dogs
barked in the distant. The bleating of goats pierced the
quiet capital. The mourning period for King Uzziah was
complete; after reigning thirty-nine years, mostly in forced
isolation, the king had died and was buried next to his fathers. His son, Jotham, who had acted as co-regent was
now king in Judah.

Khaliut bowed. "I wish you a long and prosperous
reign, King Jotham," he said, two days later, when he could
obtain an interview with Judah's new king.

"Thank you, Sir. My aides tell me that you are from
Cush," Jotham said. "By the looks of you, I had thought
you from Mizraim."

"Yes, many have made that mistake, Sir," Khaliut said.
The king motioned for him to continue. "For your safety,
Your Highness, I would like to reiterate the information I
have given to your staff about the young man. I believe he
is a royal reporter for Assyria, with hostile intents toward
Judah."

"Yes, he has been detained for questioning. The lad
worked for my father, King Uzziah."

"Gathering intelligence?"

"I am afraid so, but I believe his loyalty lies with Assyria."

"You have lost him, Your Majesty." The king raised a
brow. "I just saw the lad exiting the city gates."

"He has managed to escape?" Khaliut nodded yes. The
king turned hard eyes toward his staff. Two soldiers bowed
in unison, before running from the room. "Whom do I
thank for these warnings, Sir?"

"I am Prince Khaliut, grandson of King Kashta of Cush and Upper Kham."

A reverent hush fell in the king's court. King Jotham stood and took Khaliut's hands. "Prince Khaliut, I regret to tell you that a message has arrived in Judah this day. You must return to Cush at once, your grandfather, the king, has died."

***

Mother is coming. Nekhti ran her hand across her swollen abdomen. *When Khaliut added on this extra room, he was certain that we would have more children by now.* She walked to the living area and took one last look around. *Not the finest place in Napata, but it is the biggest house in this village.*

She set her best ivory vase on the dining table, and filled it with water and branches from a date palm that was loaded with small, green fruit.

I wonder what brings Mother to Napata. She has never visited. Neferua stopped by briefly, during the emergence season, but she left straight away. She was ashamed to be seen in this village, as am I.

What do I say now? Khaliut has promised our departure for seasons now. And I have quit asking. My neighbors think me silly, telling them constantly that we are to leave, but never doing so. She put a hand on her forehead. *How embarrassing. I had never thought I'd live like this.*

She heard a knock at the door. Nekhti went to the window and peeled back the matting. Her mother was there, looking around the village with a horrified expression. Nekhti let her in.

"Welcome in peace, Mother."

"In peace, Nekhti," she said coming inside. Nekhti took her trunk from her and hauled it into the spare room.

Then she came back and reached out for her mother's shawl. Kerit-Amon readjusted the blue shawl about her shoulders, then placed a hand behind her ear. "Where are the children?"

"I have but one. A son. He is out tending the fields."

"Only one? Why?" Kerit-Amon sat on the two-seater couch.

"Khaliut is rarely home."

"Who cares for your crops?"

"Khaliut has workers to tend the fields when he is not here. Where is Neferua?"

"I have no idea. She comes and goes as she pleases." Kerit-Amon took a wide glance around the room.

Nekhti ran her hands down her dress, then sat next to her mother. "How is Father? Did he not wish to travel with you?"

"No."

"I hear that he has returned to farming." Her mother made an indistinguishable sound. Nekhti changed the subject. "What brings you to Napata?"

"Our great king is dead, Nekhti. Or have you not heard? I have come to visit friends and mourn the Hawk at Gebel Barkal." Her gaze fell on the ebony chairs, ivory vase, and cedar dining table. "You have nice things, Nekhti.."

Nekhti choked. A compliment. From her mother. She breathed deeply, preventing tears from coming to her eyes. "Thank you, Mother. Khaliut brings me things home from his travels. Peace offerings, I suppose." She stood. "Can I get you some refreshment, Mother? I have palm wine, beer and mint leaves to brew?"

"You have wine?" Kerit-Amon looked at her daughter oddly. "How can you afford wine?"

"I do not know. Khaliut insists on it."

"And where are your servants?" Nekhti shrugged. "You have a strange setup here Nekhti. Your farmer lives like a prince and a pauper. Have you met his family?"

Her mother voiced the concerns she had been feeling. "No. His mother lives in Waset and does not wish to travel to Cush."

"I will take some wine. Your home looks better on the inside than it does on the out. We will see we what can be done about that." Kerit-Amon stood and removed her mourning shawl.

***

The Kurru district, long the burial place for Cushite royalty, was disrupted this morning by the clamoring of several gold-plated chariots. When the royal family had disembarked, a small crowd had formed. The family all dressed in blue for mourning, moved slowly inside the flat-topped entryway. A steep-sided pyramid stood directly behind.

The air felt cooler inside the sepulchral chamber. The family stood in silent reverence, watching the priests' complete funerary rites, sealing King Kashta's trip to eternity. The monarch's body lay on a blue-glazed bed. He wore linen garments, the same sword that had brought him victory in Kham, was set between his thighs.

Furniture, jewelry, gold, frankincense, and myrrh surrounded the bed. The king's favorite horses had been mummified and placed in a separate burial chamber. Bearers came in with the king's favorite leather sandals, toiletry items and Senet game board.

Forming a semicircle around the king's mummified body were the Queen Mother Kasaqua, Queen Pebatjma,

Princesses Tabiry, Peksater, Khensa, Nefrukekashta, Merit-
amon, and Abar.

The Crown Prince Piye stood at the head with his
brothers Shabaka and Miamon. Pebatjma placed a lotus
blossom wreath on her husband's chest. Prince Shabaka
ran his finger along the bed's frame. Piye stared at the departed king, willing him to rise.

***

When General Lemersekny arrived in Napata just before noon, the town was still in mourning. A lone man, rid-
ing atop an elephant, passed the general going in the
opposite direction. Lemersekny could see the flattop
mountain of Gebel Barkal, but thought it strange to see no
one outside Napata's foremost temple. Not for long,
though. Soon the city would be filled with well-wishers
and dignitaries from afar for Prince Piye's coronation.

As the morning sun dimmed and midday arrived, even
the noise of children at play was not heard.

Lemersekny had accompanied Kashta and his sons to
Kham against Osorkon. Cush and the Wasetian clergy continued to rule the Southland, and the minor Libyan princes
reigned in the north.

The general's chariot pulled up alongside the royal palace. He was ushered inside by the royal guard, then led
down quiet corridors by a barefoot female servant. The
general, too, moved stealthily down the castle's halls.
Though the seventy-two day mourning period was complete; he was careful not to disturb the still reverent atmosphere.

The solid limestone castle had cone-shaped towers with
an audience room in the center, and several apartments on
each side. Pillars etched with alphabetic inscriptions sup-

ported the palace's many balconies. The servant passed the
War Room and led the general to the door of the first audience chamber.

"Your Highness," Lemersekny said to Piye. The incoming Royal Hawk nodded to him. The general bowed
his greetings to the two princes and senior officers, before
taking a seat. An aide opened the door and ushered more
guests in.

"Royal One, live forever," Katep said. The newly ap-
pointed High Priest entered, followed by his priestly asso-
ciates. They bowed to Piye.

"Welcome, friends."

Katep sat opposite the new king, while his assistants
took seats near the staff. Piye had his father's snub nose
and receding chin, but his mother's sharp eyes. Hawk eyes.
Penetrating is the word that came to Katep's mind, the kind
of eyes that could see through limestone walls.

"Again, Sir, allow me to offer my condolences over the
loss of your father, the king. He worked tirelessly to form a
strong Waset. However, my friends in Men-nefer tell me
that the throne is far from secure, and that you should be
concerned about a certain Libyan lord."

"Are you referring to this Tefnakte?" Piye said.

Katep flashed a grin at the disdain in the Hawk's voice.
"Yes, Sir." He waited for the royal to speak more, but Piye
watched the High Priest with quiet stillness. "Rumors ab-
ound that this Tefnakte's ambitions are not limited to the
delta." The High Priest looked around the room, gauging
the level of support from Piye's staff.

Piye stole a glance at his brother, Shabaka. With a
struggle, the incoming king suppressed a grin at his younger sibling's feral expression. Piye turned his attention back
to the priest.

For his part, Katep found it difficult to relate to Piye.
Perhaps a different approach would prove fruitful.
Piye raised his brows and said. "Do you have any other
concerns, High Priest?"
"None, Sir. I think you will be pleased with our contri-
butions to your coronation. It serves Kham well to see a
son of Ham take his legitimate place on the throne. We
have made every consideration for a successful transition."
"Good, but let us not get before ourselves, High Priest.
My influence remains in Cush and the Southland, as was
my father's."
"True, Sir. May I remind His Majesty of our ancestor
Narmer-Menes. He launched a war similar to your father's;
the renowned Southerner brought Upper and Lower Kham
under one crown. And if I may be so bold sir, I hope it is
the ambition of this house to do the same. Our ancestors
would expect no less."
Piye smiled slowly. "Well said. Though there are
many goals I would like to accomplish during my reign, a
needless war and loss of life are not among them. Do not
despair. I believe the time will come when Kham will again
be under one crown."
Katep descended from a long line of priests. The Wasetian clergy knew how to manage monarchs. Proud ones,
greedy ones, stupid and insecure ones. They bowed to the
will of the clergy, sooner or later. Katep did not know what
to make of the oldest son of Kashta, but he would figure
him out. He stood and bowed. "Until tomorrow, then.
Life, health, and strength to the Royal Hawk. And may the
House of Alara never die."
"Live forever," his fellow priests intoned.
Piye's eyes followed the clergymen as they left. The
room was quiet after the Wasetians departed. Piye turned

to face Pamiu. The Grand Vizier nodded. *He* understood
the incoming Horus-on-the Throne perfectly.

***

Princess Tabiry watched as the servant showed her several gowns for tomorrow's coronation. *I do not like Kham.
And I do not like Khamites. An arrogant brood. Five hundred inundations of bondage they have given us, their
brethren.*

The servant, seeing her mistress' fierce expression,
placed the green silk aside and selected another. *Why
should we help them now? Let the Libyans take over their
land and plunder those ridiculously large eternal dwel-
lings.*

A tap on the door interrupted Tabiry's tirade. The servant with the gowns was getting nowhere with her mistress,
so she happily rushed to the door. Another servant entered
with three ebony containers filled with jewelry. Tabiry
pointed to the gown she wanted, then selected matching
bracelets, rings and necklaces.

"Your hair, my lady," said the servants who had carried
in the jewelry.

Tabiry rose and went to her gold-coated dressing table.
She reached for her bronze mirror and watched as the ser-
vant's nimble fingers wove briskly in and out of her hair.
"That style will do well," she said, startling the servant.
"But I will wear my wig in the evening." *Lest those snobby
Khamitic women think me half-dressed.*

"Yes, my lady."

*Anyone without a plaited wig was considered out of
fashion.*

"Ugh…" Tabiry moaned aloud.

The servant jumped, afraid that she had pulled at the lady's scalp too hard.

"No, do go on. My thoughts are sour this day."

The servant exhaled. "Yes, my lady."

***

Prince Shabataka, seven summers old, looked to his right at the throngs of people who lined the route; then to his left to watch the women dance and cheer. Napata was rarely this boisterous, or this crowded.

The prince did not understand the meaning of the revelry. He did, however, notice its seriousness, for he was dressed in full royal attire. A skullcap covered his shaven head. He was wearing his good sandals, the gold ones.

The youngster looked up at his father. Piye had on the Sparrow-Hawk crown, the one his grandfather Kashta had worn before he soared into the heavens. His sister Qualhata's hair was decorated with colorful ribbons. Her head was buried in their mother's shoulder, an attempt to shield herself from the noise.

Shabataka turned his attention to the boys who ran along side the royal caravan, trying to keep pace with the horses. The chariots turned and headed toward a large, flat-topped mountain. The prince knew they were at their final destination, Gebel Barkal. He knew that his father would now take his grandfather's place. That meant he would no longer have time to race toy crocodiles with him. Or take him hunting.

Prince Shabataka reached up for his father's hand, pleased that the Royal Hawk of Cush grasped it with his.

www.ingramcontent.com/pod-product-compliance
Lightning Source LLC
Chambersburg PA
CBHW030636130626
46552CB00002B/885